NIGHT OF HAPPINESS

TABISH KHAIR

PICADOR INDIA

First published 2018 by Picador India

First published in paperback 2018 by Picador India
an imprint of Pan Macmillan Publishing India Private Limited
707, Kailash Building
26, K.G. Marg, New Delhi - 110 001
www.panmacmillan.co.in

Pan Macmillan, 20 New Wharf Road, London N1 9RR
Basingstoke and Oxford
Associated companies throughout the world
www.panmacmillan.com

ISBN 978-93-86215-63-5

1 3 5 7 9 8 6 4 2

Typeset by R. Ajith Kumar, New Delhi
Printed and bound in India by
Replika Press Pvt. Ltd.

Praise for *Night of Happiness*

'A riveting page-turner' *Deccan Herald*

'A metafictional novel that wears its self-consciousness lightly, at no narrative cost' *Hindu*

'Tabish Khair's latest novel is a deep dive into the seemingly quiet, mundane lives marked by the horrific violence of the Godhra riots' *Hindu BusinessLine*

'A story about Hindu privilege as much as it is about the "invisibilization" of Muslims in India, this is a taut work … that packs a punch' *Hindustan Times*

'A taut navigation of faith and the shrinking space for dialogues in India today' *Indian Express*

'Tabish Khair's new novel takes a chilling look at trauma and Muslim lives in India … Khair is deft in probing into the psychological recesses of his characters' *Mint*

'A novel of quiet intensity' *Open*

'A slender, brisk narrative … The book leaves a crumb trail of discomfiting questions about what it means to be a Muslim in contemporary India' *Scroll.in*

'[A novel of] timely relevance' *Telegraph*

'A serving of distilled wisdom' *Week*

For Ammi

This is how it begins ...

You enter the room.

Who are you?

You could be anybody. Maybe you are a businessman or a CEO, passing through this teeming North Indian city, and staying for a night in one of its five-star hotels. You could be a prosperous doctor attending an international conference, or an ordinary tourist from Denmark or the US, splurging on this room for a night or two after tramping the heat and dust of Indian streets. You could even be a writer, put up in this hotel – the sort you cannot afford on your own – by the organizers of a well-funded festival.

Or you could be a hotel employee, of the junior-management sort, sent in to check that the bar is fully stocked, or the cleaners have done their job –

someone from another part of India, say, Manipur, or Kerala, or Bengal. But, no, you cannot be a mechanic, ordered to repair the air-conditioner, or the cleaning lady. That is not a possibility in this time and place. You could be *almost* anybody.

It does not matter who you are, as long as you are the kind of person who can pause and read in English, or why you are here in this five-star hotel room. What matters is that you open the first drawer of the glass-topped teakwood cabinet next to the bed, the drawer in which copies of the *Bible* and the *Bhagavad Gita* are kept. There, under the copies of these two books, seldom read in this room, you discover reams of paper filled with a minute and neat handwriting.

You take out the sheets, perhaps only to throw them away. But your attention is caught by the first page: there is a title on it that intrigues you, partly because it has been crossed out. And then, there is a stanza that you might vaguely recall from your schooldays.

It is a manuscript of some sort.

The writing reaches out and catches you by the sleeve. You feel its desperate tug. You start reading …

~~THE SPECTRAL INFINITUDE OF SMALL DISTANCES~~

They groan'd, they stirr'd, they all uprose,
Nor spake, nor moved their eyes;
It had been strange, even in a dream,
To have seen those dead men rise.

1

The sky had been a deep blue some hours earlier, but it was a gunnysack now, grimy and weighted with rain. Just Ahmed and I were left in the office, as was usually the case on such late evenings. And exactly when Ahmed was making the last of a dozen confirmation calls to our partners in Dubai, the storm, which had been a growl in the throat of the sky, burst with a deafening flash of paparazzi lightning.

I felt bad for Ahmed. Not only would he be late, he would get drenched too. I knew he never carried an umbrella. He never carried anything except that stainless-steel tiffin carrier, wrapped in a clean cotton towel. He always spread out the towel on his desk and carefully arranged the three steel containers of the tiffin carrier on it before commencing to eat.

He carried nothing else. He did not even take work home. He simply stayed on and finished it, sometimes working past midnight. He was the only one of my employees who could be asked to work on any day, which he often was, as I ran an export/import business. The bigger it grew, the more we had to work according to the calendars of other nations and cultures. Holidays seldom coincide across borders. But if a deposit had to be made in Damascus during Diwali, I could count on Ahmed to stay back and take care of it. If a shipment had to be counterchecked in Iceland during Eid, Ahmed was willing to do so.

Any day he would stay back without a murmur, without a frown. Any day, that is except this day.

It was Shab-e-baraat. Ever heard of it? I hadn't when I first met Ahmed, but then the only Muslim boy in class at my boarding school spoke English with an Oxbridge accent. It is not one of the Eids, the one with the sacrifice or the one with the sewai. Those I knew. Those my Muslim classmate used to celebrate too: once his parents had come down and taken us all out to the house they would rent just outside Shimla, where they were throwing an Eid party that year. Friends and family had flown in and motored up from all over. It was like a Diwali party, minus the fireworks, plus the sewai desserts. But Shab-e-baraat?

Ahmed had told me about it during his first year with us. But I guess I should begin by telling you how I came to meet Ahmed.

I had just started the business, after a stint of teaching at IIT, based on my MBA from the same institution and then a PhD in Business Communication from Columbia. Total waste. Teaching. Academia. What a shitload of pretension and monotonous meetings! Babble, boredom and bad pay. I had had enough within three years. The missus quite liked campus life though; we had met at Columbia, where she had been sent by her Mumbai-based family to do a master's in Creative Writing. Those days she was still writing a novel, and rebelling against her father's millions. I guess the two were the same thing.

Anyway, I took a loan from my father-in-law in Mumbai and a bank whose directors knew my father, and went into export/import, as they say. Best decision of my life, though my wife came round to it only after we started making very good money and she graduated from writing novels to organizing literary soirees. The money helped in the latter endeavour.

But in the initial days, before the moolah started rolling in, I had just three full-time employees. Ahmed was one of them.

I recall interviewing him. I had been surprised by his age. He was forty-two years old then; somehow, I had not noticed his year of birth on his résumé. That made him around a decade older than me, and I remember feeling awkward in his presence. He already had grey hair. Clean-shaven and with a way of looking at you directly in the face. Not hostile, but disconcerting. An austere face, deeply lined, with deep-set, almost unblinking eyes. Dressed in clean, well-ironed clothes, which were not entirely the cut or colours that were in, so that he reminded you of someone from an older generation. That was Ahmed.

I guess I had called him for the interview because of his name – he was the only Muslim applicant. Oh well, I thought, now I bloody well have to. But I was also prepared to reject him. Honestly, I had almost made up my mind to reject him. I did not want to feel prejudiced by not giving him a chance, but I had never known a Muslim intimately, and, well, you know how it is in such matters. One wants to work with known factors. First rule in business, first rule in life: work with known factors.

So I looked at him, a thin man, about four inches shorter than me – but then, I am a bit over six feet – and I prepared myself to go through the ritual of interviewing him before sending him a kind rejection slip. He was competent, not brilliant but evidently efficient. He had experience too, of the kind of work I wanted to recruit for, though not here – he had worked in other places, mostly at a multinational's warehouse and office in Mumbai and their branch office in Surat. He had moved here some months ago, he told me. Why? He looked at me, without blinking: 'I needed to move.' I was taken aback by the terseness of his reply, and mentally ticked a box on the negative side for him.

But just as I was going to say thank you, we will get in touch with you, a small, previously overlooked section of his résumé caught my eye. 'Languages spoken.' Under it he had listed not just the usual English, Hindi, and in his case of course Urdu, but also Marathi, Gujarati, Bhojpuri, Bangla, Arabic, French, German, Thai, Tibetan, Japanese and 'a smattering of Chinese'.

Initially I was sceptical. That many? So varied? How was it possible?

Ahmed had a story about it. He had grown up in a small town called Phansa, not very far from Bodh

Gaya. In high school and all through college, he did odd jobs to help his mother. He was an only child and his father had died in a train accident when Ahmed was two or three. His mother, a religious person who strictly observed the purdah, had sent him to school, taking on all kinds of sewing, knitting and embroidery work to supplement the small 'widow pension' she got from the government. As soon as Ahmed could – which was when he entered secondary school – he strove to earn some money, mostly by running errands for neighbours.

One of the neighbours moonlighted as a tourist guide. There were not that many tourists coming to Phansa, but Bodh Gaya – you know that is where Buddha attained enlightenment; when was it, some 2,500 years ago – well, Bodh Gaya would get tourists from all over. I should know: my parents had taken me there in my childhood and then I had returned much later, bride in tow, or maybe it was the other way around, for it had been my wife's idea to visit the three main Buddhist spots of India that winter vacation.

Ahmed later told me that he even met Richard Gere strolling around in Bodh Gaya one day. At that time, he did not know who Gere was, but the self-possessed man in faded jeans was identified to him by a friend as a 'famous film star from America'. That kind of place, you know; just imagine what would happen to Richard Gere if he walked down a road of this city!

At first, Ahmed had started working for the neighbour in Phansa, mostly because he spoke and understood English far better than others in the mohalla. He must have had an ear for languages, for he was going to a government-run zilla school, not an English-medium convent. Soon the neighbour started taking him to Bodh Gaya during the weekends.

The place opened Ahmed's eyes: an entire world was there, in that sleepy little hamlet. There were the Tibetan refugees and the Buddhist monks, but there were also tourists of all sorts: Thai, Chinese, Japanese, Sri Lankans, Germans, Danes, you name it. 'The place also opened up my ears,' Ahmed told me that day at the interview. 'Some of the regular guides knew other languages, particularly Thai, French, German and Japanese. I found it surprisingly easy to pick up languages. I already had Urdu and Arabic from home. Ammajaan had insisted on my learning these two at the neighbourhood mosque, and I had Hindi and English from school. But within weeks I was picking up entire phrases in other languages.'

By the time Ahmed finished high school, he was spending all his weekends and vacations in Bodh Gaya.

He loved taking people around. He had a studious bent, and read up on the history behind the place, its famous Mahabodhi temple and the ruins around it. This gave him an advantage over many other guides, who often depended on hearsay or inspiration. The other advantage was his flair for languages: the more languages he picked up, the more tourists from those cultures sought him out.

Soon he was earning more during a good weekend than his mother did in a month. People are generous when you speak to them in their language. They are nicer, happier; 'Their hearts unlock a room for you in their distant homes.' This very statement gave me reason to rethink, because of course it would also work in the export/import business.

But I was still sceptical during the interview. Did this man really speak all these bloody languages? His English was good, I could hear that, not convent-accented, but clear, correct and idiomatic. There was evidently a lot of reading behind it too. But Thai? Japanese? I was intrigued. I asked him to be prepared to come back another day. 'I want you to speak to a Japanese acquaintance of mine who will be in town later this week,' I told him.

I had not expected Ahmed to return. But he did, when I finally fixed the appointment, and he conversed with Mr Kimura. I could see that Mr Kimura started off warily, his impassive business face barely managing to conceal his amusement, but within minutes his guard was down and the two were chatting like old friends. I did not understand a word, but I did not need to; it was evident that Ahmed was fluent in Japanese.

When Mr Kimura came home to have dinner with us later that day, he joked about it. 'Your interviewee,' he said, 'if you don't want him, I will take him. Why, he sometimes uses lingo that I never thought they taught in Japanese classes! I could use his linguistic skills.'

But so could I. That is how I hired Ahmed, and soon he became my right-hand man.

As I watched it pour and Ahmed finished his last call, I felt a twinge of conscience. There was so little this man had asked of me – not even for a raise, though naturally I had given him many raises over the years. He was still my right-hand man, even now when my business had sixty-seven full-time employees in more than a dozen cities and four countries. And he still stayed up or stayed on any time I asked him to do so.

The only thing he had ever asked of me was this one holiday. Shab-e-baraat. 'It is the night of happiness,' he had explained to me the first time we had spoken about it. That, as I told you, was in his first year with me.

We were in the old office, in the suburbs. I was in my shirtsleeves, peeling an orange. It was around ten at night and we were having trouble with a consignment in Germany. 'Too late now,' I told him. 'Even the Prussians must have pulled down the shutters for the day. We will have to do it tomorrow.'

That is when he said it: 'Tomorrow is Shab-e-baraat.'

I was still thinking of the consignment. 'Something in Germany?' I asked him.

He gave his faint, slightly sad smile. 'No, no, Mehrotra sa'ab, it is a Muslim festival. We celebrate it.'

'But I thought you guys celebrated Eid,' I said from my desk, automatically offering him an orange segment.

He accepted it with a nod, and put it in his mouth. He chewed slowly. By then I knew him well enough to wait: he never spoke when eating. Actually, I suspect he never did two things at the same time. He was old-fashioned and slow in that sense, no multitasker. He always finished a task before moving on to the next one.

After he had swallowed the pulp, Ahmed finally answered me: 'This is a smaller festival. It means the night of salvation: Shab-e-baraat.'

The word 'baraat' caught my attention.

'Your wedding anniversary?' I asked him. I knew he had a wife. It was on his résumé: no children, but a wife.

He shook his head, looking bewildered. Then he understood. 'Ah,' he said, 'Mehrotra sa'ab, because I said "baraat"? But you know, "baraat" means so many things: innocence, tryst, salvation, happiness.'

I did not know. So, the wedding processions we took out were called happiness? I had to remember to tell the missus later that night. It was the kind of thing she liked to know.

Ahmed continued: 'Shab-e-baraat is a bit like the Jewish Yizkor, though we have it only once a year. A full moon day of devotion and celebration in the month of Shabaan.' He always had these bookish references in his conversation, not that I knew any more about the Jewish Yizkor than I did about the Muslim Shab-e-baraat in those days. 'During Shab-e-baraat, we recall our ancestors, those who are dead, the ones gone before us to the realms of eternal peace and joy, the ones who made us possible on this earth. It links the past to the future through our present. That is why for me it means the night of happiness. We visit the graves and burn incense there – though some Muslims are refusing to do so now because it is considered un-Islamic. And, of course, we make halwa at home.'

Halwa I knew everything about, though I did not know that like sewai, it was associated with a festival too. I guess every traditional dish is associated with some festival or the other! Even the pragmatic Protestants in my alma mater had their turkey, though often it used to be dressed-up chicken, for Christmas. Not to mention the Christmas pudding.

'Tomorrow, Mehrotra sa'ab,' Ahmed was saying, 'I would prefer to stay home. Shab-e-baraat is the only festival that matters to me.'

Then, probably feeling he owed me an explanation – we were still new to each other – he added, 'You see, Mehrotra sa'ab, ever since Ammajaan passed away, my wife and I have always celebrated Shab-e-baraat together. We cannot go to Ammajaan's grave – she was buried in Phansa – but my wife makes halwa and we consecrate it, pray for peace as is the custom and spend the evening together. It is a kind of family tradition between the two of us now: my wife makes this delicious maida ka halwa taught to her by Ammajaan. I grew up eating that dish. No matter how poor we were, Ammajaan always made that maida ka halwa for Shab-e-baraat.'

I am not sure I have managed to capture the tenor of his response. It was politely worded – Ahmed was always courteous; one thought of that Urdu word associated with Lucknow, 'adab' – but for the first time I sensed something like steel under all that satin. What was it, the way he looked at me, unblinkingly, or the way he spoke, enunciating his words even more clearly than he usually did? It sent a sliver of unease through me – perhaps what you would feel if a loaded gun was pointed, playfully, at you. Then, being the obliging person he was, he relented. 'I could come in the morning but I will leave around noon.'

I had allowed him to take the day off that year – after all, the Germans could be expected to speak English – and every year after that. Until this year.

With the financial slowdown making all of us jittery and a truly huge order on the line, I had requested him to come in, promising to let him go around three. And we were now three hours over the deadline: it was after six in the evening. I would call him a cab, and he would reach home in half an hour, I thought. I had already resolved to give him a substantial perk for this day's work. He could still have joined his wife for the halwa celebration in the evening, but for this storm.

I called all the taxi services we used, but they were either booked or not running. The buses wouldn't be either. I cursed myself for driving to office this morning, but the missus had needed a driver and the second driver had reported sick. I could see Ahmed look worriedly at the sheet of water pouring down outside the windows, the roads filling up with rivulets. The wind was growing louder. Internet and phone connections were already unstable.

Then I thought: why don't I drive Ahmed home? He could give me directions, and I would still make it to the five-star dinner to honour some literary prize winner the missus had lined up for us. Who knows, maybe the literary dinner would be called off anyway. I could not imagine writerly types of the sort the missus associates with getting their embroidered sari edges and handmade trouser bottoms wet in a deluge.

In any case, I had time to drop Ahmed before heading home.

He did not object, though he looked distinctly uncomfortable. 'If you can get through, tell your wife that we are on our way,' I said to him.

'No need. She will be there,' he replied. I glanced at him, surprised at the flat certainty of his words and tone. It was as if he was passing an ominous judgement, not making a simple statement.

Later, after I experienced what I did, I turned the phrase over and over in my head.

She will be there.

2

The rain spoke with greater harshness in Ahmed's part of the city. There were too many roofs, and no gardens or parks to soften the sounds. There were sheds, tin kiosks and squatter shanties, now seemingly abandoned, on the sides of the roads. The billboards were many, and metallic.

It was a waterfall pouring out of the skies that evening. The wind was like an animal in pain; the thunder made even me think of the voice of the gods. It was easy to imagine cavemen discovering the gods in such a storm! Branches had been torn from the few trees in the neighbourhood. I had the wipers on at full but still had to clutch my steering wheel and peer over it through the windscreen. I had not seen another vehicle on the road for the past five minutes or so.

Something that looked like a newspaper came flying towards my car – a new Toyota Innova, bought less than a year ago – and I swerved just in time to avoid it when I realized it was a sheet of corrugated metal blown off some shanty rooftop.

'We are here,' said Ahmed, pointing to a gate on the left. It had an asbestos-roofed guardhouse next to it but no guard. The gate was open; its panels, chained to iron poles on both the sides, were bulging and banging.

I turned tentatively into the gate and the apartment buildings it led to: the level was lower there, and about a foot of water had accumulated in the driveway, making it look like a narrow canal. However, the parking lot was raised a foot or so above the driveway. Thin rivulets of water were crossing the lot, but it had not been submerged yet.

It was a typical lower middle-class apartment complex, of the sort built by public corporations in the 1970s. A dark, cavernous parking lot on the ground floor, with insulated wires looping across pigeon-infested corners, and four or five storeys of two- or three-bedroom flats, with pokey little balconies. It was the kind of neighbourhood that often makes me feel sad and uneasy. I once had an experience like that in the US. A foreboding man suddenly loomed across my path, stuck out a large paw with grimy fingernails, and asked for money. Two dollars, he was exact about that, a man dressed in rags, layers and layers of discarded clothing, his face raw and red. But he was a giant of a man, bearded and bristling with hair, and his gruff voice – two specific dollars – was impossible to read: was he begging or threatening? I had felt pity and fear, and had dropped him a dollar, not because I could not afford two, but because I needed to find a way to maintain my self-respect. That is how I felt about such neighbourhoods too; they seemed to exude a mix of sadness and threat.

I parked the car as directed by Ahmed. He had been looking worried all along the drive. I attributed it to his being late for whatever ceremony he performed with his wife for Shab-e-baraat. When he had first talked about the halwa made for the festival, he had mentioned something, somewhat apologetically, about consecrating it. 'I am not religious or irreligious, Mehrotra sa'ab, but ceremonies are necessary to live in a fuller world than this one,' he had said.

Now he got out of the car, carrying his towel-wrapped tiffin carrier, cuddled on one arm like a baby, and hesitated, a hand on the open door. There was a strange expression on his face, as if he was torn between contrary impulses. He bent down to look at me. 'You should not drive back alone in this storm,' he said.

The thought had crossed my mind too, especially after the car escaped being slashed by that metal sheet I had taken for a newspaper. But I did not want to be stuck here.

Ahmed added, as if reading my thoughts, 'A storm like this at this time of the year – it cannot last more than another ten–twenty minutes.'

Then he gave his slight, sad smile, his face clearing up. 'Mehrotra sa'ab, come in for a while. The storm has reached its peak, it will abate soon. Have a cup of tea.'

Why not, I thought. Even the missus can't blame me for being delayed by a downpour.

A narrow corridor, lined with tin mailboxes on one side, half of them broken, led to a narrower flight of stairs in Ahmed's building. His flat was on the fourth floor, he told me. There were two flats on each landing, some of them with a potted plant, which had once been hopeful, next to the door, a couple with brass name plaques, others bare and unadorned. It was obvious that there was no lift.

Trudging up the stairs, which had a stream of water cascading down one side of it from a leak further up, Ahmed apologized to me on behalf of his wife. 'She observes the purdah. I will request her, but she might not come out to meet you. When I was younger I tried to talk her out of it, just as I once tried to talk Ammajaan out of it.' He shook his head in recollection and added ruefully, 'I failed.'

'Well,' I said, trying to be polite, though I was a bit taken aback by the revelation, 'it is part of your faith, isn't it?'

'Depends,' replied Ahmed. 'Depends on how you interpret it, Mehrotra sa'ab. I have never heard of purdah as the sixth pillar of Islam!'

I knew it was something he felt strongly about, strongly enough to talk about it on occasions. He seldom talked religion otherwise. But I had overheard him discuss it in office with some of the others. I had read about the five pillars of Islam in school textbooks, but it appeared to me, from the news that I read now, that the pillars had been multiplied by a few hundred in recent years. Wasn't jihad one of the pillars too, now? But I did not have to reply, as we had reached his flat.

Ahmed did not knock. He let himself in with his key. At that moment I thought nothing of it: Ahmed was the kind of person who never bothered anyone, never asked for favours – pass me this, fetch me that, please – and I assumed his wife would be busy cooking the halwa in the kitchen. Ahmed had told me that the main trick was to pour in the sieved flour, the other ingredients and milk and stir them at an unhurried pace on a low fire, before adding the melted cardamom-infused sugar while still churning the mix. Later, it struck me as unusual that he had not knocked or rung the doorbell, and that the door had been locked with a key rather than latched or bolted from inside.

The storm had already relented – I could tell from the sounds. But I could hardly turn back and leave from his doorstep. It would have seemed most impolite. I followed him in. Did I really feel that I was stepping into another medium, a denser, slower one, something more resistant, as when you dive into the swimming pool, or is it a thought I associate with my entry into the flat only now?

The door led straight into a sitting-cum-dining room. It was the usual sort, I guess: a sofa, two chairs, a low table in between, a couple of lamps with cloth shades on corner tables, and behind this section a small dining table with four chairs around it.

One window had been left open, and even though it was netted with wire to keep mosquitoes and flies out and the balcony it opened onto was partly sheltered, the rain had washed in and was lying in a pool under the window. 'You forgot to shut that window,' I remarked. I could not possibly have said, 'Your wife neglected to close that window,' could I?

Ahmed looked at it and replied, after a moment of hesitation, 'I always leave one window open. To seal a space is to shut out a soul.' Strange sentence, isn't it? Like a line from a poem, cryptic, pithy, but what did it mean, what could it possibly mean? I did not pay attention to it at that moment – we knew in office that Ahmed spoke like that at times – but later, yes, later, the line came back to haunt me.

To seal a space is to shut out a soul.

With a courteous gesture, Ahmed placed me on the sofa and hurried through the curtains of one of the doors into what I presumed was the kitchen, telling me in English, 'I will see if she needs help with the chai.'

I looked around. There was a large laminated poster of puppies with the usual mushy slogan – I forget what – above the sofa, and two photographs on another wall. One of the photos was of an old woman, and I did not have to be told this was Ahmed's Ammajaan. The resemblance was clear, if difficult to pin down. Maybe it was in the eyes, the steady stare, that look which said, with resilience not hostility, 'I know you, but I do not hold anything against you.' Or so I remember thinking. Why did I think of it as 'but', not 'and'? I have no idea, but later, when I went through every moment and thought I experienced in that strangely bare sitting-cum-dining room – and you will understand why when I tell you what happened – I always came back to this particular thought with that specific conjunction: 'I know you, but I do not hold anything against you.'

The other photograph was even easier to place. It featured a younger Ahmed and a woman wearing shapeless but colourful clothes. It was obviously a wedding photo, clicked in a small-town studio, as could be induced from the false 'Swiss' backdrop. What caught my eye was not the photograph or the fact that Ahmed could actually look happy, unabashedly happy, but the wife: she had a Mongol-like look. Not Chinese or Tibetan – they are usually fairer – but maybe Nepali or Manipuri. Dark, but with more Chinese than North Indian features. I was surprised. I knew Ahmed's wife was religious, even orthodox, unlike Ahmed, and I had assumed he had married one of his own community – maybe even a cousin as Muslims are reputed to do. But this woman with her round face, her high cheekbones, her slanted eyes, her dark but ruddy complexion: she could be no kin of Ahmed's!

At that moment, Ahmed came out of the kitchen and caught me looking at the photograph. 'The day after our wedding,' he said. 'But you have no idea how much I had to argue before she allowed me to put the photo out here. And to think she had never even covered her head until the day the photo was taken! But Ammajaan – I guess I have to blame her, I have to blame dear Ammajaan for the fact that my wife refuses to come out and sit with us even today.'

He joined me on a chair next to the sofa. 'Another five minutes, she says,' he added. 'Though you will excuse me for serving you no halwa; it is not ready yet.' Then he started, as if he had heard something, and said, 'No, no, don't worry; Mehrotra sa'ab has to leave soon.' Obviously, he was replying to his wife in the kitchen, though I had not heard anything, perhaps because the storm had not died down completely.

But as he sat there, ears pricked one would say, as if listening to his wife again, I tried to pay attention, and all I heard was the sound of the dying rain and a TV in a neighbouring apartment. Ahmed shook his head seemingly in mild amusement and, excusing himself, went back to the kitchen.

Ahmed was a soft speaker, and I could hardly hear him as he conversed with his wife in the other room. But I did catch a few words of what he said to her:

'No, not necessary ... You don't understand, Roshni ... Oh well, as you wish then, as you wish.' All of it in Hindustani, of course. Strangely, his wife must have been whispering, for I did not hear her at all, not above the squabble of a saas-bahu serial coming from the TV set next door.

Perhaps she kept her voice veiled from strangers too? I tried to not give much thought to it, refusing to heed the murmur of doubt. And in any case, I was more intrigued by what Ahmed had revealed about his wife and their wedding, and I could not help questioning him when he returned, shaking his head slightly. 'You mean,' I said to Ahmed, 'your wife had to convert to marry you?' I thought of what had been in the news recently: 'love jihad' is what those Hindutva lunatics called it, and while I disliked their fervour and terminology, I could not – deep in my heart – totally accept the fact that Muslim men married our women and converted them to Islam. The marriage bit I did not mind, but the conversion? That made me uncomfortable, maybe even a bit resentful. I won't pretend otherwise.

Again that faint, slightly sad smile. 'You see, that was the problem,' Ahmed replied. 'That is what finally forced us to move to Mumbai.' But he did not really answer my question. He did not say his wife had to convert. I thought that was what he had conceded, but no, he did not say it – as I realized later.

Ahmed went into the kitchen again, this time to fetch two cups of tea, in cheap flowery porcelain, of the sort you buy from general stalls with stuffed shelves. (I know: that is the sort of crockery my wife buys for the servants to use.) The tea was much sweeter than what we drink at home. Then, as we sipped the steaming hot brew, he explained: 'Roshni – that's my wife's name – never really knew what faith she had grown up in, and I never asked her to convert. Everyone else around us did, of course; we lived in a mohalla. And when I married her nevertheless, everyone we knew put pressure on Ammajaan to get Roshni to convert. All those uncles and aunts, who had for years given us the occasional Eid gift but pretended not to really see Ammajaan's hardship; even her regular clients, the contractors and affluent families for whom she had stitched and woven, all of them wanted Roshni to convert. All of them wanted Ammajaan to press me. But, for some reason, Ammajaan did not do so. She said to them, "Roshni is a Muslim name, isn't it? She says her mother was Muslim. This is a Muslim girl. How can a Muslim convert to Islam?" Maybe that is why when Roshni came into our house, she imitated Ammajaan in her routines, even down to observing rigid purdah. At first I protested – she had never worn a veil, no, far from it – but how could I prevail against two determined women?' Ahmed laughed, a laugh that was little more than a grunt. 'You see, when Ammajaan passed away, it made no sense for us to stay on in the mohalla. The neighbours had not accepted Roshni. Neither had anyone from my family, apart from Ammajaan. Mumbai made better sense. A big city. We could start anew there. Little did I imagine …'

Suddenly, as if a switch had been thrown, there was darkness on Ahmed's face. As if a curtain had fallen. His face closed; it simply shut down. It happened so abruptly that I almost looked around, expecting someone to have entered, to have caused that change. But there was no one there, just me and familiar, transparent Ahmed, now worryingly opaque, as if something had come between us, something heavy and brooding, like a monsoon cloud.

I waited for Ahmed to resume, but his account had petered out, as the rain outside was petering out too, and he seemed lost in thought for a few seconds. His face assumed more creases and shades, as if an invisible artist was reinforcing lines drawn in the past with deeper strokes. Then he shook himself out of his reverie and glanced at the curtain segregating the kitchen. 'Ah,' he announced, 'it is ready now, and I have to do as I must. What do we all do but what we must, Mehrotra sa'ab? You know, Ammajaan taught this recipe to Roshni. Roshni makes it exactly as she used to. Can you smell it?'

He sniffed appreciatively – or was it anxiously? – and got up. It relieved the atmosphere of brooding expectation that had settled on us when Ahmed had abruptly discontinued his narrative. He collected our cups – we had finished our tea by then – and, placing them with his trademark slow care on the plastic tray, took them back into the kitchen. I sniffed discreetly. There were food smells in the air, but they could well have been from adjoining flats – there was nothing distinctive about them. I prepared myself to be enthusiastic about some insipid fare, which is the usual burden of being served a dish someone else has grown up with.

This time Ahmed was gone for longer. I squirmed impatiently. The rain had diminished to distinct drops now, and I could hear traffic on the streets again. There had been no thunder or lightning for some time. I texted the missus to say that I was on my way but delayed by slow traffic because of fallen branches and wires.

Ahmed came out of the kitchen carrying the same plastic tray, but now it held two small plates and two glasses of what, from the colour of it, seemed to be Rooh Afza. I detest that nauseating drink, and have never understood why so many people swear by it. Is it even real rose extract, I have often wondered.

Ahmed handed me a glass of Rooh Afza first. I accepted it gingerly, gazing dubiously at its contents and wondering how to get out of drinking it without offending anyone in the flat. Ahmed, I knew, would understand; he was not easily offended. Actually, I had never seen him offended by any incident or remark. But the rose drink must have been prepared, like the halwa, by his wife, and I did not want to seem rude and spoiled-rich to her. The best thing, I thought, would be to take a sip or two, and then just let it sit on the table, as if I had forgotten about it. I proceeded to bring the glass close to my lips, blocking out its overly sweet and synthetic smell, and forced myself to sip from it.

So engrossed had I been in negotiating the Rooh Afza that I had not even glanced at the plate Ahmed placed in front of me. He had gone back to his chair, holding his plate, and was eating from it. I put down my glass and picked up my plate. It was then that I noticed it did not contain any halwa. There was a pile of nimkis and a small spoon on the plate, but no halwa.

At first, it just struck me as an omission: Ahmed may have simply forgotten, in his hurry not to detain me longer than necessary, to put halwa – that famous maida ka halwa he always talked about – on my plate! I was going to bring this to his notice with a joke; I glanced up at Ahmed, who was busy eating. My jokey remark was aborted by the sight of the plate that Ahmed was holding. There was no halwa on it either! Only, as was the case with my plate, a pile of nimkis and a stainless-steel spoon.

Can you imagine how taken aback I was? Yes, the sense of foreboding returned at that instant: It is one thing to forget to put something on a plate you are serving and another to not notice its absence on your own plate! Time slipped back, just a few minutes, to that moment when I had seen a shade fall on Ahmed's face.

But, still, I felt only discomforted, confused; it was nothing compared to what I experienced the very next second, when Ahmed, with the gentle tinkle of spoon on china, scooped 'halwa' out of his plate and levered it, carefully, making sure nothing spilled, to his mouth. It was then that I broke out in a cold sweat: Ahmed was totally engrossed in 'eating' the halwa! I felt as if a cold gust of air had entered the room, and folded around my neck like an icy muffler. I stood up, half stood up anyway, and if Ahmed had not been so absorbed in eating the non-existent halwa, he would have noticed it. I sank back into the sofa, eyes riveted on Ahmed.

He put down the spoon, picked up a nimki, dipped it in the part of the plate that was bare, and then carried it to his mouth. He chewed, he swallowed. Then he grasped the spoon again, this time to scoop up empty air from the vacant part of the plate and 'eat' it, his jaws and throat muscles moving exactly as if he was chewing and swallowing. I was filled with a sense of horror, horror of the sort I had never experienced or imagined.

At that moment, Ahmed looked up from his plate and saw me staring at him, my plate inert in one hand. A vulnerable expression flickered across his face, some emotion raw and indecipherable. Then he gave his slow smile and said, 'Go ahead, Mehrotra sa'ab; you have not touched it. I promise you, it is delicious. Exactly as Ammajaan used to make it. If anything, even a bit better!'

What could I do? What could I have done? How could I tell a person who was eating ghostly halwa that my plate did not contain that food either? I picked up a couple of nimkis and popped them into my mouth, that icy muffler strangling me now, my fingertips cold and numb.

'No, no,' said Ahmed, 'try them with the halwa. That is the best combination.'

I picked up a nimki and dipped it in my plate, as though using it to scoop up some halwa. Then I carried it gingerly to my mouth. I put it in and chewed slowly, doubtfully, which Ahmed probably took for appreciation, for he looked pleased, relieved even, and nodded before returning to his plate. I could feel the nimki in my mouth, but of course there was no taste of halwa.

Ahmed's calmness, so domestic, so normal, must have defused my sense of icy horror. The chill that had gripped me, filled me with numbness, subsided. But now I felt bewildered, angry and insulted. I did not then know the source of these emotions, especially the anger and feeling of humiliation, but I have since turned that moment over and over in my mind, and I comprehend them better now.

Bewilderment anyone would understand. But I felt anger too at the situation, at Ahmed, for turning out to be so different from everything I had taken him to be. Until then he had been the most reliable, reasonable, trustworthy and easy person I had ever known. Now suddenly, he was – what was he – demented, superstitious, crafty, crazy, a fool? In any case, he was not the person I had known. By not being what I thought he was, he had thrown my world out of gear.

A motorcycle was being kick-started under the building.

And the insult? Yes, I was humiliated, because I felt forced; I felt I had to act a role. What would happen if I were to say, Ahmed, you are crazy, there is no halwa on our plates! Would he go bonkers and start raving and arguing? Or would he laugh and say it was just a joke on me? Which would be disrespectful too, that sort of liberty taken with someone who paid his salary. Also, what if this was not just some hidden craziness, but a deeply subconscious bid of Ahmed's to humiliate his boss? I could not know. I did not wish to know.

Time had slowed down even further in that tawdry flat with its pool of water next to the open window. The seconds and minutes were flies and tiny insects stuck on the edge of a cauldron of boiling molasses, which is one of the images that have stayed with me from the only time I visited some remote villages while backpacking along the Ganga with my Columbia University batchmates.

It had stopped raining outside. Entirely. I heard the water dropping from roofs, gurgling down pipes. It sounded ominous, as if the world had gone hollow. The place seemed filled not with real sounds but echoes, ghosts of dead sounds.

I decided to play along with whatever it was: madness or a sadistic game. I needed time to think. I swirled a few more nimkis – at least they existed and tasted good – in the empty halwa part of the plate and popped them into my mouth. I even drank the Rooh Afza in my distraction and hurry to finish off the nimkis.

Then I put the plate down and made my excuses. I was late; the missus was waiting for us to go to a dinner.

Ahmed looked slightly disappointed. 'It was too rich for you, wasn't it?' he said. 'You left most of the halwa untouched.'

I made appropriate non-committal noises. I could not force myself to say something complimentary about the halwa, so I asked him to thank his wife for the 'snacks'.

Suddenly the place had filled with too much … too much of what? I could not make up my mind. I felt that each fat drop landing with a plop on the dingy balcony outside and the ledges of the windows was heavy with clouded significance. The water I could hear rushing down pipes and cisterns spoke a language both expressive and incomprehensible.

'I need to rush, Ahmed,' I told him. I need to kick-start time again, Ahmed, I wanted to scream; I have to free the minutes from the molasses of your rustic cauldron!

Ahmed was polite as always. He insisted on accompanying me to the car. As we left the flat, I stole a glance at the kitchen, and the curtain moved slightly, as if his wife was standing behind it, listening to us.

3

The missus was not actually thrilled. The girls had been sent up to their room with the ayah almost an hour back. I had ignored two or three urgent text messages while driving back. The fact that when I reached home the storm had ceased outside, but increased manifold inside my head, did not help. I was distracted, inattentive, trying to make sense of what had happened in Ahmed's apartment. Luckily, I did not have to chauffer us to the dinner – the other driver had been retained by my wife – and it was a short drive.

The dinner had not been cancelled, and we arrived an hour late. We were by no means the only people to arrive late. The storm had delayed others too, not least the deputy minister and the senior writer who were the guests of honour. Even the five-star hotel people were running late, righting the potted palms that had been knocked down in the driveway, mopping rainwater from the lobby, setting the hall. All this assuaged the missus, as did the fact that she was instantly surrounded by a group of young and aspiring writers, all dressed either like Bollywood stars just back from Hollywood or like models doing an ethnic show.

It allowed me the time I needed to compose myself, put in place a face to meet all those faces.

The hall was set for a buffet, two sides lined with silvery containers, some simmering over small flames, some still being installed. There were high round tables, without stools, on one side of the hall, close to the food tables, and chairs and sofas on another side. In the sofa-and-chair section of the hall, against a wall bearing a large poster featuring the cover of a prize-winning book and exclamatory blurbs by famous writers, there was a low purple-carpeted dais with a mike, standing bereft of speakers at the moment.

Uniformed bearers were circulating with trays bearing elaborate snacks and drinks. The light from chandeliers, fashioned like strings of diamonds, was reflected off the real and false diamonds adorning many necks. Not my wife though – she only wears pearls to literary events.

I had verified the dinner's raison d'être from my wife on the drive to the hotel. Evidently, a British writer of Indian origin had won a major award and, as he was in town en route to a festival in Hong Kong, this dinner had been thrown by his Indian publishers 'to felicitate a son of the nation', as the publicity pamphlets scattered around the hall put it.

The son of the nation was, as far as I could see, standing surrounded by a lot of admiring daughters of the nation (and a couple of other nations) in one corner of the hall. This being only his second trip to the country, as the missus had informed me, he must have arrived on time, and was now waiting for the deputy minister and the senior writer to make their appearance. The storm was not the reason those two were late; they would have been the last to arrive in any case. The son of the nation still had to learn the national trick of arriving fashionably late, I thought.

All this provided me with the time to consider what had happened in Ahmed's flat and to regain a bit of composure. Until then I had been filled with something like a sense of dread and gnawing distrust. It was the feeling of someone who had been walking on what he thought was solid ground and had discovered it was only a thin crust of ice over a deep chasm.

Something had to be done. That much was clear to me. I have always been a man of action, and I take some pride in thinking logically. Success in business, believe me, depends a lot on thinking clearly and rationally. I took a pakora from a passing waiter, dipped it into the green chutney on the tray and bit into it, ironically thinking of what a relief it was when things were exactly what they seemed. The sheer solidity of this hall and the people in it pleased me immensely at that moment.

Yes, I knew something had to be done. But what? Should I confront Ahmed? Should I ask him to explain? Should I simply fire him? For, of course, I could not trust a madman to run my business, despite the fact that until now he had been my lieutenant. I knew that the success of my business owed almost as much to Ahmed as it did to me, but it would be foolhardy and bad policy to simply overlook what I had experienced in Ahmed's flat. A man so troubled as Ahmed obviously was could go bonkers all of a sudden, mess up a major deal, or even walk into the office with a gun one fine morning. I could not ignore it. I owed it to my other employees, to myself. I owed it to my business.

And yet I hesitated to confront Ahmed, or summarily fire him. To dismiss him so quickly, so unthinkingly, appeared a trifle unjust to me. I am not an unjust employer. In Ahmed's case, moreover, I knew that I owed him much; I had come to care for him, as one would care for an older friend. As far back as I could think, in the old office and now in these larger, glitzier premises, I recalled innumerable evenings of the two of us working alone, in our shirtsleeves, late into the night. I could not think of lunch breaks without picturing Ahmed at his desk, the towel spread on it to prevent any spill, the steel containers arranged almost geometrically on the towel. He always ate alone, in his cubicle, and almost never went out with the others for lunch in the neighbouring South Indian eatery, and yet no one considered him unfriendly. We just understood that the lunch hour was his moment to be alone; for the rest of the time he was the one person all of us could, and would, ask for help. I thought of those occasionally pithy sentences he would utter, lines that the others called Ahmedisms. Here's an Ahmedism from last week, one would say: 'Rain is a relationship of the earth to the sky.' Here's another, someone else would remark, as Ahmed might shake his head and give his sad, slight smile: 'All distances are infinite, except those of the heart.' No, I could not just fire him; I had to know more.

But I also shied away from confronting Ahmed: there was such an aura of vulnerable self-respect around him that one hesitated to say harsh things to him. He was not the sort of person anyone would jovially slap on the back or argue aggressively with. Ahmed never indulged in such acts, always treating others with the utmost decorum and old-world respect (always using 'aap', never the familiar 'tum', not even to the boy who fetched tea), and only an outright boor would take liberties with him.

These were the thoughts occupying me when the missus wended her way back to me, accompanied by a couple of young writers she was championing that season. A cluster had entered from the main door, and I could spot the deputy minister and the guest of honour, a much-awarded writer from Delhi, in the thick of the throng. They were similarly broad-faced, heavy-girthed men in their seventies, fair and of medium height, dressed in almost identical ethnic garb with long silk scarves around their necks; from a distance they looked like twins to me.

My wife took me by the arm and hustled me to one of the sofas, as the cluster gravitated to the dais. Florid speeches were made, but mercifully – perhaps because it was a function organized by a commercial publishing house and not an official institution – they were short. The son of the nation was presented with a heavy plaque by the deputy minister, who spoke more of the need for sports and health in India than of literature, perhaps because a cricket series was on, or perhaps because the cover of the novel – a collage of different images including a cricket bat – made the politician assume it had something to do with sports. The publisher spoke of how the book had again reinvented magical realism – that explained the collage, I supposed – decades after Salman Rushdie. 'To explode the narrow reality of our world and fill it with a universe of worlds, what work of literature can hope to do more than that?' she demanded rhetorically, conferring the honour of such an intergalactic explosion on the son of the nation.

Much as I had enjoyed reading magical realist novels in the days when I still had time to read, I felt a prickling of irritation at this remark, as I was still obsessed with my evening at Ahmed's and I could not help wishing no one had exploded the narrow reality of my world. I wondered how the publisher – or any of the other appreciatively nodding heads, coiffured and collared, including that of the missus – would feel if they were forced to eat a plate of non-existent halwa after the speech.

We were neither the first nor the last to leave. As we were leaving, I turned and looked at the people still remaining in the hall, and the thought – strange as it was – crossed my mind: could I spot someone like Ahmed in that crowd? Yes, I was beginning to be obsessed by Ahmed.

I remember surveying the crowd for a full minute before hurrying to catch up with my wife, who was being charmingly escorted out by her writer protégés, and I remember saying to myself: but there is no one like Ahmed here!

It was not really true. There were people who were Ahmed's height; there were people who were dressed like he often did – in trousers and a light coat, with a carefully double-knotted tie at times; there were people with his close-cropped woolly hair, some who were as thin as him. Two or three even had his kind of face or his slow gait. But I remember thinking that not one of them resembled Ahmed.

I hurried out to the lobby, oddly disturbed by this absence of Ahmed in the crowd I had just quitted. What was I thinking of? Why did it make me sad? I did not understand it. Or if I did, I misunderstood myself at that moment, attributing the sadness to the insularity of all our worlds: the literary world has always reminded me of the academic world that I had dabbled in, or the corporate world that I frequent, large bubbles of talk unintelligible elsewhere, though of course my wife disagreed strongly the one time I made this comparison. Literature is about all of life, she had argued, and I knew she was right, but it never changed my impression.

As we waited for the car to be announced and driven up, I thought of the distance we would drive, back to my house, and the distance from my house to Ahmed's colony, and though the two were roughly the same in kilometres, they seemed entirely incommensurate to me. The car drove up. It was the Toyota Innova, which being the newer of our two cars is the one the missus takes to such functions. I knew I was not thinking clearly and made an effort to pull myself together as a turbaned and moustachioed doorman held open the door of my car for my wife and me.

4

The next morning was clear, azure sky and all, sunlight falling through the gaps between the curtains like solid golden bars. By the time I went down, the girls – seven and ten years old – were already in their school dresses and dutifully spooning cornflakes under the watchful eyes of their ayah and the missus. Usually, I am the first person to get up in the family – apart from the servants, of course. I no longer need to: my business is a well-oiled machine, run on rational lines which enable all of us to see a problem coming and sort it out in time. I do not captain a business that lurches from crisis to crisis, and if we are hit by a small disaster then it is of the national or global sort, not anything of our own doing. Those crises – the national or global sort – do affect us, and have been getting a bit thick on the ground in recent times, but we manage to cope with them: my staff has learned from the calm and level-headedness that I and my lieutenant in the main office, Ahmed, always display. So there is no reason for me to get up early, but it is a habit, and, honestly, most mornings I almost leap out of bed. Even in the days when I read novels, I could never finish any by authors like Dostoevsky or Sartre.

There are people who take time getting out of bed. My missus, for instance; she lies morosely awake for at least half an hour before leaving the bed. But I wake up and am out of the sheets within a minute. I have always been like that. I cannot wait to get started. I believe it is because I run my life (and business) on clear lines; I have no reason to dread getting snagged by the unexpected during the day.

Not that morning. I had not slept well. The night had been full of dreams, mostly faded now, of which the one I still vaguely recalled in the morning (perhaps because it had recurred) featured a hand detaining someone – me, I thought – by the sleeve. There had been something familiar about that dream.

I lay in bed for almost an hour, well after my wife

had quit it. She asked me if I was well and I mumbled that maybe I drank a bit too much at the dinner last night. It was a lie; I never have more than a glass or two. She gave me a quizzical look, but then went into the girls' room to supervise their school-going. We have been married long enough not to quiz each other too much.

I rang the bell and asked a servant to fetch me a couple of the day's papers and a cup of karak tea. We subscribe to all the top papers; it is on the office tab, and I believe in following the news, not just the business pages. Then I stayed in bed, pretending to read the papers and sipping tea. There was a great reluctance in me to get up, and I knew it had to do with a mix of repulsion and trepidation: I did not want to reach my office and encounter Ahmed again. I wanted to forget what had happened last evening. I knew I could not. And I knew I could not ignore it either, especially when confronted with Ahmed's presence in office.

Would I detect signs of madness in him, a glitter in the eye, a fervour in the voice, a grasping of the hand, or would he still be as he had been for so many years: polite, considerate, orderly, reliable?

As you can imagine, I reached my office late. Ahmed

had already held the morning briefing in our meeting room – it was his job in any case, though I usually liked to be present – and all the staff (except one who was on leave as she had a wedding to attend in Kolkata) were back in their cubicles.

I wished to steer clear of Ahmed that day, though I knew it was not possible. But I tried to avoid meeting him, and closed the door to my office. I am the only person in the place to have a separate office, but I always leave my door ajar unless I am having a meeting. By leaving the door ajar, I think I signal my availability to all my staff: anyone can walk in with a matter. When the door is closed, the assumption is that I am holding a meeting or, for other reasons, do not wish to be disturbed.

That gave me a bit of breathing space. I switched on my computer and checked my email, answering a couple. I checked on shares and other matters. I perfunctorily read the reports sent in from other offices. But all these were mechanical acts. What I was really thinking of were the dreams, half-remembered, from last night, and, inevitably, the plate of nimkis – without halwa – at Ahmed's flat. The more I thought of the plate, the more unreal it seemed to me. If someone had walked in and said to me, 'Ah, you are back from Toronto – how was your trip?' I would have welcomed it as the real explanation and slotted the experience at Ahmed's flat as a bad dream I had while flying back! I was that desperate to wish it away.

Then the thought struck me: this was so uncharacteristic of me! I was trying to hide behind stories, to construct fictions, instead of facing facts. I asked myself: how are facts faced? I knew the answer: facts are faced with evidence, with data, with numbers. Fiction cannot be numbered; it cannot be proved. But facts, yes, I have known it all my working life, I have built my business on it – facts can be proved.

In Ahmed's case, I argued with myself, I could not get the evidence on my own – there was too much between me and him, too much humanity, too much reciprocity, and I needed someone else to collect the evidence for me.

I knew exactly the person for it – Devi Prasad of the Prasad and Sons Private Investigations Agency.

Why hadn't I thought of it before? Maybe because I did not wish to get Ahmed investigated? But I had used Devi Prasad and his agency on numerous occasions: often to check out potential business partners, once to pin down a corrupt employee. And then, in a flash, I could place the familiarity of that dream of the hand reaching out and detaining me by the sleeve. It was nothing. Just the shards of a memory jogged by a discussion of Coleridge at one of my wife's literary dinners some weeks ago, lines from a poem I had once memorized for an elocution contest in school. It was the ancient mariner detaining the wedding guest. I laughed aloud with relief.

I wonder whether you smile at this because you recognize the compulsive nature of the account I am penning down here, how it ignores everything else for just one story?

Devi Prasad's agency is not one of those cubicles in the wall you might associate with private dicks. It is swanky, like a multinational corporation's showroom, its reception staffed by a beautiful North-eastern woman dressed in impeccable corporate gear, down to the tie, and it is in one of the more expensive parts of the city. Not everyone gets to meet Devi Prasad, who looks more like a prosperous CEO than a private investigator. But I had no trouble getting admitted to him: I was an old client and we played golf together. Or rather our kids did – we had children about the same age, though Devi was a bit older than me – as our respective wives had decided the kids had to play golf. So, once a week, we took them to the club, where an instructor put them through their paces, while we reclined, drink in hand, on wicker chairs outside the club restaurant. This was expected of us, as fathers. The mothers took care of the chore on the other golf-training day of each week.

Devi Prasad was surprised I had come to see him in his office. He was an astute man and understood it must be something vital. Motioning me into one of the plush leather chairs against his mahogany desk, he closed the door behind us, after instructing his peon not to let anyone disturb us. Then he returned to his swivel armchair, seated himself in it and simply looked at me, the fingers of both hands touching at the tips and gently fluttering. He was wearing a waistcoat – Devi has a penchant for them and two-tone shoes, season permitting – and his clipped goatee gave him the look of a solicitous dentist. Why a dentist? Perhaps because I could imagine him extracting information as cleanly as a dentist would pull out a tooth, and sending off just as elaborate and large a bill!

Faced with his fluttering fingers, I was a bit lost for words. I could not possibly tell him about the invisible halwa and Ahmed's incipient madness. Devi knew Ahmed, having met him during functions, the last time when we celebrated my company's tenth anniversary at the Radisson. I had also sent Ahmed to Devi's many years ago, when I was getting another business checked out. I never sent him again, as it was the only time Ahmed had explicitly disagreed with me.

'It is not something for me, Mehrotra sa'ab,' Ahmed had told me after the visit.

'What's not for you?' I had asked, quite uncomprehending.

'Suspicion, maybe,' he had replied. 'I am not the suspicious type. I do not want to be involved in suspecting others.'

'But, Ahmed,' I had reasoned, 'we need to know everything in order to trust our collaborators.'

He had smiled his sad smile. 'What does knowledge have to do with trust, Mehrotra sa'ab?' he had almost murmured in reply. 'There is no *need* for trust if one has knowledge.'

I had not understood his reluctance, but I respected him, and I never sent him for similar jobs to the agency. I took care of future cases myself, and as such built up quite a close relationship with Devi, further cemented by the last few years of paternal golfing.

Yet, I could not force myself to tell Devi about the evening at Ahmed's flat. It was partly because I was afraid of sounding stupid; Devi, like me, was a highly practical person. I also felt I owed Ahmed – who was so careful of his own space – a degree of reticence, at least until there was concrete reason to abandon it. I had brought a copy of Ahmed's résumé. It had been updated over the years, as was my policy with all senior employees. I instruct them to make 'all relevant changes' in their résumés every March, and resubmit them to me using encrypted files.

I put the printout on Devi's desk. I could not bear to mention the name, so I simply said, 'I would like to have this person's domestic and personal circumstances investigated.'

Devi picked up the file and opened it. Then he glanced up at me, surprised. 'Ahmed?' he asked, and then added, inevitably, 'Ahmedji?'

I nodded.

He put the file down and looked straight at me. 'I thought he was your right-hand man,' he remarked.

'He is,' I replied.

Devi frowned. 'Embezzlement?' he asked.

I felt embarrassed and guilty. 'No, no,' I hastened to assure him, 'nothing like that. Ahmed will never do anything like that, you know. It is just that …'

But I couldn't really tell Devi, could I? What would he think? Wouldn't he just burst out laughing and perhaps regale all of us at the club with a wicked account of it some New Year's Eve?

I made up a story instead. 'Ahmed's been distraught.

Not acting like his usual self. I think he has problems at home. Maybe his wife is ill or something. I want to know what his circumstances are, so that I can help if necessary. I cannot ask him directly. You know him; he has so much self-respect. I just want to find out. I don't want him to find out about it though.'

Devi laughed. 'You are an even better employer than I thought you were,' he said. 'If I cared half as much about my people, I would go crazy.' Was there a touch of irony in his words because he only half-believed my explanation?

He dropped my file in a drawer and added, 'No problemo, boss. Consider it done.' He liked to say 'No problemo, boss' to all problems; I suppose it was his version of 'Elementary, Watson.'

Devi Prasad and his people are nothing but efficient. That is why they have the reputation and the clientele that they do. He called me five days later, on my mobile as we had agreed.

'You don't really have to see me, boss,' he said on the phone. 'There doesn't seem to be anything much, apart from one discrepancy, but I suspect you will want to follow it up.'

We agreed to meet at the golf club that afternoon. It was not one of our chaperoning-the-kids days.

There was a time one could sit in the restaurant of the club and hold a private conversation. My father had been a member, and I remember coming here with him during the two periods he was posted in this city. Only a few members and the occasional guest would be there, and members mostly left you alone with a nod. It was a very British atmosphere, even in the 1980s. Then the Indian economy changed, more Indians started feeling the need to belong to elite clubs and swing a golf club; membership exploded. As the restaurant continued to be one of the best and cheapest places to eat in, members began bringing in guests. Soon the place was congested. And as the members and their guests wanted to meet and greet people – the club's restaurant was no longer a place where you avoided the undesirable over a whisky or met the chosen over a meal – it became impossible to hold a table without being greeted by all kinds of acquaintances all the time. The only way one could have a private conversation now was to go golfing, which is what Devi and I did. We selected a discreet caddie.

Devi waited until the second hole. Then he began out of the blue, 'The subject, you know … nothing remarkable. A quiet man, respected in the neighbourhood as he seems to be quite helpful despite being quiet, lives alone.'

That's the kind of stuff I had been expecting. What kind, I did not know, but something like that, something normally odd or oddly normal that could explain the unexplainable. I looked up; I tried to appear surprised. Devi was preparing to swing. He did not notice the expression on my face.

'You had asked me to find out about his family circumstances, but there aren't any. His résumé mentions that he doesn't have children, and that is the case. No child. Also no wife living with him.'

'The résumé …' I said helpfully, restraining myself. The explanation, give me the explanation, I wanted to shout at him.

Devi swung and the ball described a perfect curve, settling down three metres from the hole.

'Tchah,' he said, beaming with satisfaction. He continued, 'I know his résumé mentions a wife. One name only. Roshni. But she does not live with him. No one has ever met a Roshni. No one has seen her. People consider him a widower. No woman has ever been seen with him in any case.'

It was my turn now. I selected the right club and waved the caddie back.

'Divorced maybe?' I asked. We were getting there, I thought.

'We couldn't find out, boss. No evidence here; he doesn't even get guests. Never been a wife in this flat, say the neighbours. This is confirmed by the part-time maid, who goes in for two hours every day to clean up and wash dishes. Dishes and clothes for just one man, she says, nothing else. If you wish, I could have it checked out in the places he has been to, that town he was born in … what is it called … and Mumbai and Surat. But it will cost much more.'

'The expense does not matter,' I replied. The explanation would have to await another incursion into Ahmed's past, it appeared, but I was hopeful; I thought that in due course I would have an answer I could comprehend. Devi was the man for it.

Devi nodded. 'No problemo, boss,' he mumbled, a bit doubtfully.

I practised my shot a few times. I could see that Devi was thinking about something.

'There is something else?' I asked him encouragingly.

'Well, I don't know. Most of it is gossip. You see, the subject is seen as harmless but idiosyncratic: he almost never invites anyone into the flat, though he is always willing to help neighbours; he sometimes talks to himself when he goes shopping.'

'So do I, trying to remember what to buy.' I laughed.

'The subject does more than we do. He talks as if he was addressing someone else.'

I paused in my swing and raised an eyebrow at him. I had never heard Ahmed talking to himself or an invisible interlocutor.

'There's something else,' Devi added. 'You see, we do not go about shadowing people most of the time. Maybe that is what private eyes do in the West, where no one seems to know his neighbour or second cousin, but this is India, where everyone knows everyone else.' He grimaced funnily and jerked his head towards the restaurant. 'So the best way to find out in India is to go through contacts. What we do first of all is try to see if one of us knows someone who knows the subject. I have a staff of twenty-seven and each one of them has circa 227 contacts, each of whom have … well you know, it is like that Chinese legend of the grain doubled per square of a chessboard, and at the end you have more grain than the earth can hold. You would be surprised how often we end up knowing people close to the subject. We call it "getting the family lore".'

I took my swing, got the angle of approach wrong and did much worse than Devi. We started walking again.

'As you can imagine, this time we could not get the family lore directly from around the subject. He keeps to himself and does not seem to have relatives in the city. But we got an indirect connection – recycled family lore, the boys call it. The flat adjoining the subject's is occupied by an old couple; they are known to one of my men. Sen. Mr Sen's a retired headmaster. Mrs Sen's a retired school teacher. Their only son is posted in Hyderabad. Mrs Sen has arthritis and Mr Sen has other health complications. The subject often looks after them, does their shopping, fetches the doctor. You know. They love him as a son. They probably know him better than anyone else in the building. But they also said something that I am not even sure I understand ...'

'What was it?' Maybe I spoke too sharply. Devi hastened to assure me that it was nothing to worry about – 'no big deal, boss' – he was not even sure it was worth mentioning.

Devi broke off to concentrate on the shot, sank the ball, fisted the sky, and then continued: 'You see, boss, they are an old, lonely couple: Mrs Sen is so big she waddles; Mr Sen is thin and neurotic. Both are full of conspiracy theories, according to my man, who is actually a kind of nephew of theirs: JFK, Netaji, you name it. They probably have nothing to do but imagine all kinds of stuff.'

'But …' I encouraged him, practising my swing. Then I handed the golf club back to the caddie, and asked for another. I rotated my arms, lumbering up; suddenly there appeared to be a chill in the breeze.

'But they seemed to suggest that the subject keeps his wife shut up in the flat for some reason. Or so my man gathered, as they were highly vague and guarded in their wording. They spoke of her as if she existed and did not exist, at the same time. This is what made my man assume that the wife was there in the flat in some ways. Just a hunch, he claims. It doesn't make sense though, as someone, at least the part-time maid, would have spotted her. Mr Sen might have said more, but Mrs Sen shut him up with a look. My man says that Mrs Sen's looks are not to be denied.'

I pursed my lips, trying to keep a faint hammering out of my head, hunching up against the chill that I suspected only I could feel. The caddie handed me a new club. I concentrated as deeply as I could. I told myself golf is a sensible game, golf makes perfect sense. But this time my shot was even worse than the last one.

Sense was what I had wished to make of this investigation. Answers, I had expected reasonable answers.

I was disturbed. But more than that I was irritated: I felt as though Ahmed had played a dirty trick on me. You know the feeling when life seems to have stuck out a leg and tripped you without any cause? You want to kick something, scream into the void? That's how I felt.

So irritated was I at this intrusion that had upset my ordered life that, for the first time, I 'unfriended' some Facebook friends. These were not people I knew personally, and they had not posted anything particularly offensive – or not more offensive than what they had written in the past. But for various reasons – a posting on politics, some remark about Bangladeshis, a derisive comment on Obama or the Indian cricket team – I simply 'unfriended' them. A tap and they were out of my life forever!

As I did so, I regretted the fact that people were not as easy to unfriend in real life.

My way of life ... is fallen into the sere, the yellow leaf ... I recall the line from one of those plays we read in school and college. *Macbeth*, I think. Yes, *Macbeth*; I have a good memory, and my iPhone confirms it.

I had always liked Shakespeare in school and college. I was tickled by the way critics – and sometimes our teachers – interpreted him and discussed all his ambiguities and paradoxes, when actually, to my mind, Shakespeare was just finding ways out of the contradictions and impasses that he got his characters into. In his tragedies, he usually resolved them by killing off people. I thought, then, that I could see through his tricks: one of his methods was to distract the reader, or the viewer, with some powerful poetry, so that when the lazy resolution of the crisis came by – the chap in the play was blitzed by something or the other – the viewer, or the reader, was still too bedazzled (isn't that a word Shakespeare would have loved?) to notice or complain.

That line is one of those. Or was it two lines?

Anyway, the line came back to me again and again over the next few days. My way of life is fall'n into the sere, the yellow leaf ... I could feel – honestly, for the first time – the full power of that line. I do recall that this is when Macbeth has committed his crime and knows that honour and peace will be denied to him in his old age. I had committed no crime. But I felt that a crime had indeed been committed and I had been dragged into it. I did not fully suspect Ahmed of foul deeds, believe me, that was not it. I could not even believe Devi's man's wild goose theory of a woman hidden in that flat in some devious way.

The crime was more like an existential disturbance:

it denied me the peace and calm I had hoped for. Someone was guilty, and I wanted it to be proven that it was not me, because what had happened in that flat had somehow, in some vague, weird manner, imposed a burden of guilt on me too. Something *had* grasped me by the sleeve.

I wanted my days to be golden, not yellow.

5

Ahmed's father was a low-grade municipal employee, and he died in a train accident when Ahmed was between two and three. That much I already knew. Ahmed was not garrulous about personal details, but he was not overly secretive either, and given a genuine context, he would tell me things.

The context, on this topic, had been in his second year with me, when we were still a business of just four or five people. I had told him he would have to take care of our appointments the next day, as I would not be coming in. Then, because it was a day rather heavy with work, I explained to him: 'My father is flying through, and I have to spend time with him. You know, alas, the sort of thing one has to do.'

In those days, my father was on his last diplomatic posting – in Paris. My mother had already moved to the house they had bought for their retirement in Goa. She was setting it up, and writing – as she has done all through her life – colourful travel pieces for various publications. My father was on his way to spend a week in Goa, before returning for his last three or four months in Paris.

Ahmed thought about it and said, 'Mehrotra sa'ab, one is lucky when one has to do such things.' He added, 'I sometimes think of it.'

'Think of what, Ahmed?'

'I think of what it would be to have a father visit you, to talk about your small worries and joys with a father. But I am not sure I even remember what my father looked like. He was very religious and did not get a portrait done. I have only seen him in group photos, and maybe just a dozen of them. Small, stained, black-and-white photos, or photos in faded colour. He could be anyone. Ammajaan never referred to his accident or death. She only said, *he never came back*. Sometimes I think of what brings people back. Love perhaps? Not hate, I am sure of that; hate has the power to take away, not to bring back. But love surely, not love as in films, but a conversation of hearts across distance. Who knows? I suppose a point comes when no one comes back. Ammajaan did not come back either. We are rags being blown by the wind in a light drizzle. We get heavier with time. And one day we stay where we are.'

As was occasionally the case when Ahmed went into his soliloquies, I had ceased following him. He would, at times, speak in shifting ideas, as if using a few pieces of a jigsaw that only he could visualize.

So, I had known for some time that his mother had brought him up. Devi's printed report from the two men he sent to Phansa filled in the missing bits.

Ahmed's father belonged to the Tableeghi Jamait. 'This is a small but thriving society among religious Muslims, which is best understood in terms of evangelism,' the report explained. 'These are Muslims who believe that the message of the Quran has to be spread, especially among other Muslims who, in their opinion, have forgotten it. In secular terms, one can describe the society as fundamentalist, but it is both pacifist and, unlike organizations like Jamait-e-Islami, not political. They see themselves as modern, not as traditional or fundamentalists. Their stress is on education and living an ethical life defined by Islamic precepts. While they insist on strict purdah in public, they also encourage women to get an education and seek respectable work.'

After being widowed, Ammajaan was not abandoned by the local members of the society. She was provided with support, mostly in the form of work such as knitting, stitching, weaving, some of which she had done in her spare hours in the past too. While she paid for Ahmed's education in the zilla school, society members took care of teaching him Arabic and Urdu. He went to a local mosque for his lessons. He was brought up as a proper little Muslim in the mohalla.

I can imagine Ahmed at eight or nine, skullcap on his head, scampering along the narrow alleys of the mohalla – it was called Maruganj, said the report. I can imagine Maruganj. (Is it a gift that I have always had, or has it come to me, come to me after …?)

I tell myself I can imagine Maruganj because I have been to Muslim mohallas in bigger, older cities – Old Delhi, Agra, Lucknow, Hyderabad – mostly as a tourist, inspecting the old mosques and forts, being taken through long, winding, filth-filled alleys, avoiding the eyes of the beggars or hurriedly dropping them a coin.

Maruganj in Phansa must have been dingier, dirtier, its alleys narrower, its sewers uncovered and overflowing, bearded men sitting in corners, children in skullcaps, shrouded women, the stench of decay and filth everywhere except when, suddenly, a different smell would drift by – the fragrance of burning incense or an appetizing whiff of one of the many kinds of kebab being skewered over an open fire. I have no objection to beef – neither did my father, though my mother was and remains a vegetarian. I can appreciate the smell of beef kebab, and its taste.

Strange, isn't it, incense and kebab – those are the good memories that I associate with my cursory incursions into Muslim colonies. Smells, memories that travel in the wind, as if they carry, encapsulated in themselves, the history of a people who have moved, and moved, and moved. The missus would wax eloquent on this; she discovered Sufism – through a translation of Rumi – at Columbia, and has ever since been an enthusiast of that branch of Islam, ignoring my, at times provocative, remarks that it seems to have little to do with Islam as practised and enunciated by mullahs today. 'What do you know?' she would say. 'Well, I read the newspapers,' I would reply, holding up a sheet and pointing to some report of an Islamist atrocity or terrorist attack. There was always one handy. She would throw up her hands, half comically, as she knows I am only half serious when I make such remarks, and go on with whatever she was doing.

Those smells, and then suddenly, through devious, grimy alleys, strewn with filth on the ground and caged by electricity and telephone wires overhead, a sudden glimpse of some exquisite dome or gateway. That is how I imagined the Maruganj that Ahmed grew up in – but, of course, I knew it would have no exquisite dome or gateway. Those are to be found in the old imperial cities. Phansa wouldn't have them. Maybe a white-washed dome with pigeons fluttering around it, maybe a decaying brass-studded door in what was left of a haveli, and the smells – that was it. Phansa was a taluk town in a godforsaken state. It was not Lucknow or Old Delhi.

I had been reading the report in bed. I did not want to read it in my office, and I knew the missus never looked at any of my business files. The only time she enquires about the business is when she needs sponsorship for one of her literary events: that is when she asks about my 'close' business associates. It is a small price to pay for privacy.

My wife came in, having checked on the kids. She was wearing a silk kimono; she had taken to wearing kimonos as nightdresses this year. Last year it had been a ghagra-choli set, adapted as a nightdress by one of her designer friends. I sometimes wonder how she can fall asleep in some of these dresses. But I guess women like to be dressed well even in bed, and the missus has retained her figure despite two pregnancies.

Don't misunderstand my tone: we have the best of marriages. A sensible one, a marriage that works. We do not bother each other with deep existential issues: just as I would not discuss the matter of the missing halwa with her, she would never moan about approaching menopause to me or the fact that she once wanted to be a novelist. We talk of small matters: the girls and their schooling, the dinner next weekend, where to go next summer. That is why I appreciate her and she appreciates me. What is far more important, we leave each other alone at times, coming together when required to maintain a sane household, bring up balanced kids. We have different interests, but both of us know how to live life sensibly. That is the trick.

The missus got into bed, looked at the file lying on the bedside table and said, 'Bringing work home again?' Just for a while, I assured her.

She smirked, playfully. 'When is the last time you read a novel?' she asked.

'Just seven months ago,' I told her. It was true. I had picked up a thriller during a vacation.

'I don't believe you.'

I named the novel.

'Well, you used to read real books when I met you,' she added, a bit ruefully.

'I used to be poor too,' I replied.

'Neither of us was ever poor.' She laughed.

'Everything is relative, ma'am,' I noted.

She prepared to fall asleep, but I propped myself up on an elbow and looked at her. She noticed. 'What is it?' she asked me.

'You have a Muslim relative, don't you?' I asked her.

'You mean my cousin's son?'

'He married a Muslim girl, didn't he?'

'Yes. Why?'

'I just need to find out a bit about Muslim cultures. Could you ask them?'

'When did you start getting interested in culture – Muslim or Hindu?' She laughed again.

I assured her this was strictly business.

'They live in Canada, Anil. And the girl is just as much Muslim as you are Hindu.'

'Of course I am Hindu.'

'Beef eater!'

'So did the ancient sages,' I argued back.

'How do you know?'

'I have read a news report on a history book on it, by a chappie called, what was it, Jha. Yes, Jha. Very Hindu name, isn't it? Brahmin name, I dare say. Your chaddi-wallahs had the book banned. Or tried to.'

'Name an ancient sage,' she challenged me.

I thought. 'Aryabhatta,' I said.

She giggled, 'That was a scientist.'

'There were no scientists in the past, only sages,' I argued back, and then added, 'Viswamitra.'

'Well,' she conceded, 'everyone can name one or two.'

'The matter that concerns me, ma'am, is not our sages but their mullahs.'

'Whose mullahs?'

'Muslim mullahs.'

'Never heard of any non-Muslim mullah.' She laughed. She was in one of those teasing moods she gets into when her literary events are going well.

'Anyway,' I said, seriously, 'I need your help. I need to speak to someone who knows Islam from the inside.'

'Not that poor girl in Canada. I will get you an expert.'

I knew what she meant by an expert: either a scholar of Sufism, or a Muslim novelist. I did not object. Either would serve my purpose.

My purpose was simple: I wanted to know more about the society – Tableeghi Jamait – Ahmed's parents had belonged to. I thought it would answer my questions. It would enable me to solve the mystery of the secluded or missing wife, the invisible halwa. I was beginning to see Ahmed as a member of some cult. But I had read only a third of the report from Phansa, and by the time my wife got her 'expert' – it was a novelist – to come to our place for dinner, I had managed to read the rest of the report. And that had changed my impression of Ahmed – and my questions – once again. Actually, as you will find out, more than just once again.

You recall my image of little Ahmed with tattered notebooks, a skullcap perched on his short-cropped hair, scampering down festering, murky alleys relieved by a flash of brilliance from an ancient doorpost or a whiff of kebab from a roadside stall? Well, as the report specified more pedantically, this image was valid only up to a certain point.

Until secondary school, Ahmed played the part of a studious lower-middle-class Muslim boy, mugging up maths tables in school and Arabic at the mosque. In his spare time, he ran errands for his mother – mostly delivering and fetching her work (saris to be mended with fine raffoo work, pullovers to be knitted, salwars or trousers to be repaired) from other houses in Maruganj, and especially from the houses of members of the Tableeghi Jamait who made an effort to provide Ammajaan with work and Ahmed with tutelage.

Ahmed was popular in school, for he was good at both English and Hindi, and popular at the mosque, where his recitation of the Quran was held up as an example even to older and full-time madrassa boys. He was not talkative even then, but he was not reclusive either – and in that description I recognized Ahmed as we knew him in the office, a man who would speak when required but would not gossip, a man who was always friendly but did not seem to have any special friends.

But Ahmed was growing. He was a boy with not just a sense of responsibility – always thinking of what he could do to help his Ammajaan – but also, hidden under those layers of mature responsibility, a child-like sense of wonder, of excitement at life, at new things, at people. In class eight – when he must have been thirteen or fourteen – Ahmed started helping out a neighbour who was neither a member of the society nor particularly religious. The neighbour's name was Hanif, and he was often called Hanif Ustad, as he was a bit of a neighbourhood goon. Hanif Ustad was not considered admirable by the Tableeghi families that patronized Ammajaan and Ahmed, but he was not ostracized either – partly because he went to the Friday namaaz and partly because he had good contacts with the kind of people who 'can get things done'. This, in a place like Phansa, I gathered, means petty government officials, policemen up to the rank of thana-in-charge, minor goons of various persuasions (and some of none), and municipal councillors. Also, the good members of the society reasoned that Hanif Ustad could hardly avoid being lax in certain matters – he was said to drink, for instance, though never on Fridays. After all, he earned his livelihood as a tourist guide in neighbouring Bodh Gaya.

The season Ahmed started working for Hanif Ustad was a bad one economically. A vague global crisis, like some jealous invisible god, had blighted businesses and salaries in Maruganj too: many members of the society had less to spare, and hence they gave less work to Ammajaan. It was this that might have induced Ahmed to start working for Hanif Ustad. Hanif had been asking Ahmed to join him for some time. 'I am very busy in Bodh Gaya during the season,' he had told Ahmed. 'You could take on those of my tourists who want to see Phansa and we will share fifty/fifty of whatever they pay.'

'Does anyone want to see Phansa?' Ahmed had asked seriously.

'Not many. But there are some loonies. I thank Allah for the loonies: they make better sense economically.' Hanif had laughed, chewing vigorously on his paan.

'Why me?' Ahmed had enquired.

'Ingliss,' Hanif had replied shortly, spitting a thin stream of paan juice six feet away into a nullah. Ahmed looked on admiringly. Ammajaan did not allow him to chew paan. Most of the society members frowned on the habit too.

It wasn't just English that helped Ahmed when he started working for Hanif. At first most of the tourists who came to Ahmed, via Hanif, were from other parts of India: very few foreign tourists diverted to see the 200- or 300-year-old temples that existed in Phansa, and rarely did a European detour to the colonial graveyard where some ancestor lay buried, having survived the Crimean War but succumbing to malaria in Phansa.

Observing Ahmed's success with the Indian tourists – which, he was canny enough to realize, depended a lot on the boy's ability to pick up phrases from their languages in just a few days – Hanif started asking him to help out in Bodh Gaya, and sometimes even escort tourists to Rajgir and Nalanda.

Ammajaan felt uneasy about this, mostly because some of her Tableeghi acquaintances warned her against Hanif Ustad's 'influence'. Did she bring this up with Ahmed? The report did not say anything about it, but I suspect she did not do much. Maybe just a word to warn him against 'bad society', I could imagine that. From the way Ahmed spoke of his Ammajaan, on the few occasions that he did, I was convinced not only of the love between mother and son but of an unusual degree of trust – the kind of confidence in the other that is built up through years of mutual support and dependence.

'Next Friday?' the missus asked me at breakfast two days later. 'Are you free next Friday?'

'Why?'

'Shuja Shirmali can come over for dinner that night.'

I must have looked mystified.

'He is a well-known Muslim novelist and journalist. Just last year he published a novel, *The Lamp of Delhi*, based on the life of Nasiruddin Chirag-Dehlavi.'

'Who is this chirag–lamp of Delhi?' I asked.

'A sufi saint, seventeenth or eighteenth century I think. You can ask Shuja your questions on Islam.'

'Ah,' I replied. 'Sure, though my questions have changed.'

My questions had changed because around eighteen or nineteen Ahmed started changing. The Tableeghi people later associated it with Hanif Ustad's influence. This might not have been the case. According to the report, by then Ahmed and Hanif Ustad had parted ways, amiably but irrevocably. Ahmed was now working as a guide on his own, and Hanif Ustad had quit the field to move on to bigger matters – an auto repair shop in Gaya, his own taxi service and municipal politics. If they met now, it was when the tourists who employed Ahmed rented a taxi driven by Hanif Ustad or his stooges.

Ahmed's reputation had grown, along with his knowledge of languages. He was now being booked before 'parties' reached Bodh Gaya, sometimes even when they were still in Bangkok or Tokyo. He was earning enough to enable Ammajaan to quit stitching and weaving for her Tableeghi patrons, though she still took on work sent her way – she felt it would be vain of her to refuse now that she did not need the money.

Ahmed did not object to it: he had not changed outwardly. He had passed the Intermediate with respectably high second-class marks, and had accepted the results uncomplainingly, though many people remarked that the only reason Ahmed did not get a first class was that there was no one to do 'pairvi' with the powerful on his behalf. He still dressed the way he had, in cheap, clean trousers and shirts that seemed just a bit out of fashion, and even the most critical of Tableeghi patrons could not accuse him of 'giving himself airs'. Many of them even sent their children to him, especially to get their English and Hindi compositions corrected, and Ahmed always found time for them.

Actually, there had been only one visible sign of change. Like most of his peers, when he finally could, Ahmed had started cultivating a small beard and a moustache. Now, at the age of nineteen, he shaved them off. This might have gone unnoticed, but Ahmed also started being irregular in attending the weekly Friday prayers. Some of the stricter Tableeghi members brought this to Ammajaan's notice, who ticked Ahmed off, but lightly because she knew his time was not always his own – he could not ask tourist parties for Fridays off, after all! Moreover, she trusted her son and, never having been allowed by society to go to the mosque for regular prayers, focused more on ordinary signs of faith and virtue: courtesy to others, respect for elders, care for the weak and children, lack of bluster about one's achievements. She could see that Ahmed remained a paragon of virtue in such matters, without even – which was just as important – considering it a virtue.

The years passed like that. There is little the report had to say of them, and my imagination baulks at filling in the gaps. Of course, I can imagine Ahmed conducting tourists through the vast, desolate remains of Nalanda, that ancient Buddhist university destroyed for perhaps being a fort by invading Muslim hordes, looted so many centuries ago. And though I wondered what Ahmed must have felt recounting that history, as a Muslim, to Hindu or Buddhist tourists – his unspoken unease, their unspoken accusation – I could imagine such scenes and even narrate them to you.

But I cannot really talk of how mother and son lived, or even what Ahmed did in his spare time. I know – the report notes it – that he had become a voracious reader. I know of this also from my experience of Ahmed. But what did mother and son talk of when they were in their rented two-bedroom section of a house in Maruganj – Ammajaan had refused to move – or when, say, Shab-e-baraat was being celebrated and Ammajaan was making the famous maida ka halwa that Ahmed had often mentioned and that, finally, was the reason for the report and my questions? What transpires in the small spaces between people covers such vast distances that it is often impossible to measure. That is what I think now, and perhaps I unconsciously echo some forgotten Ahmedism. But then?

Then, as I read the report, the questions I wanted to ask the Muslim novelist changed from page to page. Had I met him a week ago I would have asked him about the Tableeghi society, about fundamentalism and such matters – in the hope that it would help me understand Ahmed's actions that Shab-e-baraat evening when he had served me a plate of non-existent halwa. But I had read on, and I had discovered another person in Ahmed.

It was this person that created the second biggest crisis of her life for Ammajaan – the first, I assume, must have been the death of Ahmed's father.

At the age of twenty-four, while finishing his master's in Commerce at a local college, Ahmed announced to Ammajaan that he wished to get married. This was an unlikely announcement where

Ahmed was concerned. He had never said anything so decisive to his mother. The old woman, who was probably stitching a torn pocket back on a pair of jeans, put down the garment. Then she removed her spectacles and put them carefully in their case. She was astounded and overjoyed. Astounded by the tone of Ahmed's request – it was so unlike him – and overjoyed because for the past five or six years she had been prevailing on Ahmed to get married: 'I will find a nice girl for you'.

But her joy quickly turned to consternation: Ahmed had himself found the girl he wanted to marry. How had it happened to a boy as shy as Ahmed? Ammajaan probably never got the full answer, but Devi's report sketched a meeting that I could easily flesh out.

Imagine Ahmed a few weeks before he made his announcement to Ammajaan. He is a thin young man of average height, dressed in trousers and a checked shirt, sometimes a blue blazer or a green-yellow pullover (knitted by Ammajaan). He speaks various languages fluently. Imagine him walking down the roads of Bodh Gaya. It is early December, so he has his pullover on, and a cheap scarf. No, the pullover and scarf are my inventions, for the report simply mentioned that 'the following account, as reported, is ascertained to have taken place in early December.' I can imagine December in Bodh Gaya; I had taken my wife – or perhaps vice versa – to Bodh Gaya in the winter.

True, when I think of Bodh Gaya, I cannot always distinguish between my memories of the time I had visited it with my parents – I had been twelve or thirteen then – and the time I took my wife there, in the third year of our marriage, when newlyweds still go sightseeing, unencumbered by children. I had noticed a difference: the place was more crowded during my second trip, and it had a greater preponderance of bussed and chartered tourists, urbanized cafes and air-conditioned hotels, which had largely replaced the dhaba-joints, with benches and charpoys on the pavements or under flimsy awnings, and the hippie-like backpackers I recalled from my first trip. The Tibetans were still there though, the monks with shaven heads and long saffron, yellow or dark red robes, the laypeople in even more colourful dresses, traditional ones, a reminder of the fact that they had slowly followed the Dalai Lama into exile after 1959. On both the trips, I even saw some newcomers (or so I supposed they were) wearing sheepskin chubas and heavy boots, as if they had just tramped down snow-lined passages.

That is mostly how I imagine the place with Ahmed walking up its main street, every bit a small-town Indian from the plains, dressed in western clothes and a knitted pullover, his scarf wrapped around his head and neck, chafing his hands to keep them warm in a winter that is almost summer for the Tibetans. The tourist season is at its height: small shops teeming with souvenirs, statues of stone and wood, scarves, carpets, inlaid boxes; the pavement sellers hawking their spreads of Buddha heads, bead strings, incense sticks. Incense is in the air, as well as a faint stink of defecation. Further up, the Tibetan colony – a network of tents in a field – has been thriving for two months now. The Tibetans are yet to flee the heat of these plains for the Himalayan foothills, which most of them do every March in order to return after monsoon. Their return marks the beginning of the tourist season; their evacuation its end.

Ahmed is heading for their colony. He passes the many temples – all built in distinctive national styles – that line the road. Bodh Gaya is full of such temples. He catches just a faint glimpse of the Japanese temple, spare and neat, for it is a bit off the road. But he passes by the elaborately gilded Thai temple, turns left with the road, which shows a slight incline, and crosses the Tibetan temple to his left. There is a greater crowd here. Air-conditioned buses are unloading and regurgitating them. It is early evening, and a slight chill is in the breeze. A pack of street dogs run across the street squabbling; they are shooed away by two shopkeepers. Ahmed skirts the fracas.

He turns off the road, into the field where the Tibetan tents are pitched. Some of them fly banners and flags. There are mostly Tibetans and western tourists in this area, not many Indians. They are the cheaper kind of tourists: students, backpackers, some appearing to be left over from the time of the flower children. I wonder how Ahmed sees them: as 'hippies', as 'addicts', which is how I remember the locals referring to them on my second trip, or as students and ordinary job-holders out on that once-in-a-lifetime trip, a vacation in the exotic difference of India shaped by nostalgia for their own past, that time of Bob Dylan, the Beat Generation and Vietnam protests.

That is what I had found most of them to be: students out on a lark, as I too had been with my backpacking American friends when we trekked along the Ganga for three weeks, or people with insecure jobs, travelling on a shoestring. Many of them pay to sleep in the tents and eat in the Tibetans' impromptu cafes. Then Devi's report mentioned something that surprised me: Ahmed ate there too at times, though surely the meat could not have been halal. It was not just the non-halal aspect that surprised me, it was the fact that he ate there at all, for when I was in Bodh Gaya I was often warned by the locals to stay away from the 'stinking' restaurants of the Tibetan quarter. Tibetan places serve dog meat, they often appended as explanation. That is when they did not offer other, more personal, explanations.

But 'the subject had Tibetan friends,' the report stated. Devi either trains all his detectives to write like him, or has an editor working on all the reports. The latter option would not surprise me, knowing how immaculate Devi is in his waistcoat and goatee, his creaseless patent leather shoes, his way of speaking. 'It has been reliably ascertained that this was not unusual practice by the subject, as Indian guides in the said hamlet always cultivate Tibetan contacts.'

In the tourist season, the Tibetans know everything about foreigners in Bodh Gaya. It was his Tibetan friends who tipped him off two years ago when Richard Gere was in town and looking for a guide to show him the remote and unfrequented Buddhist caves across the dry Phalgu river. Ahmed got the job, and was handsomely tipped, though he recalls with some chagrin – because even as he said it, he knew he was being stereotypical, being forced by something deeply unconscious and against his better judgement to speak in an alien manner – that Gere could not help laughing when Ahmed approached him and said, 'Mr Richard Gere, I presume?'

It is one of the very few anecdotes from his days as a guide that Ahmed had ever recounted in office, chuckling drily over it.

Ahmed goes up to a tent and pulls aside its flap. His friend Thubten lives there with his family, whose exact composition and number Ahmed has never been able to ascertain. There are two sisters: sturdy, rosy-cheeked young women whose eyes Ahmed does not dare meet. They are sitting at a table – the first section of the tent is a kind of cafe, with a brick-and-mud platform running around its outer circumference. The platform, piled with quilts and cushions, serves as a bench – there are tables and folding chairs facing it – during the day, and can be rented as sleeping space for the night. A woman with dirty blonde hair is asleep in one corner, a book on yoga lying half open next to her.

Thubten's two sisters are drinking tea, made the traditional Tibetan way, with butter blobs floating on the surface. They say something to each other, and then shout into the tent for Thubten. Ahmed understands Tibetan, but they often speak too fast for him or use unusual dialect words. He knows they make good-natured fun of him.

Thubten peers in, waves a half-plucked chicken at Ahmed to indicate what he is doing and disappears again. He is bare-bodied, dressed in a pair of jeans. One of the sisters pours out butter tea for Ahmed and hands it to him. He accepts it with mumbled thanks, without looking at her. He does not sit down. He sips the tea, standing by the entrance of the tent. The girls know he won't accept their invitation to sit with them unless Thubten is there too. They giggle.

Thubten comes out in a few minutes, wiping his hands dry, and then buttoning on a cotton shirt. He likes going about without warm clothes in Bodh Gaya, as if to reiterate his origins, for otherwise he wears western clothes, prefers to speak English, and swears a lot in it. He tosses the rag at his sisters, and they exchange a few light remarks which Ahmed does not overhear, for he has finished his tea, put down the glass on the nearest table and gone out to stand by the tent.

When Thubten joins him, he slaps Ahmed on the back jocularly, and says in Hindi, 'Ahmed yaar, why are you so rude to the poor girls?' Thubten is active in the Tibetan Youth Congress and speaks Hindi fluently, though he insists he was born in Tibet.

'What do you mean?' asks Ahmed. He can see his friend is ribbing him, but Ahmed has a horror of being rude.

'You never even look at the girls.'

'In my community that indicates respect,' Ahmed replies defensively.

'I suppose in my community it would be considered rude. The girls think so, anyway.' Thubten laughs.

'I never look at women unless there is a proper reason to do so.'

Thubten is in a teasing mood. 'I thought you lot solved that problem by putting your women in those blasted burkas,' he quips.

Ahmed has a sense of humour, but this witticism is wasted on him. By the time he came to work for me, he had mostly lost the desire to defend or justify his people. He never got into the occasional arguments about Islamist terror that I overheard erupting in the cubicles of my office, answering only with accounts of personal experience – like what he did for Eid or Shab-e-baraat – when asked. It was as if he did not make any connection between abstract discussions of his faith and his own personal experience of it. At a certain point, these had become two different things for Ahmed. But in those days in Bodh Gaya, according to Devi's report, he still felt compelled to explain and defend.

Thubten, Devi's man had noted, still laughed at the recollection. (Thubten is now a prosperous middle-aged businessman, with a restaurant in Dharamsala, the report specified.) 'It was hilarious how old Ahmed would get into the intricacies of such matters,' Thubten had recounted in English over a beer to Devi's man. 'The guy was a walking encyclopaedia on his fucking faith. Oh sorry. You are not Muslim, are you? No? Thank God! I just tend to swear; I have nothing against any faith. I have a good relationship with all faiths: I leave them alone and they leave me alone. But Ahmed, my God, the man did go on and on. I think he gave me a long, rambling lecture on that occasion, quoting the *Quran* and – what's it called – the Haddis or Huddis or something, it's like a reference book on their prophet's activities, and I had just been pulling his leg. The gist of it was – I have forgotten the fucking details, oh sorry again, me and my foul mouth! – that the purdah was not a veil put on women but a curtain between private and public spaces. He had looked it up, and the veiling of women was basically just one interpretation. Another interpretation was modest dress and behaviour – and the separation of private and public spheres, which evidently had to do with something that happened to his prophet during one of his marriages, the prophet's that is, keeping in mind that the Arabs in those days were only a partly settled people. Like us, I had lightly remarked, living in tents. He had looked nonplussed and then nodded absent-mindedly. Yes, tents, he had said. I had teased him a bit more by adding that tents or no tents, if any of us tried to veil a Tibetan woman, he would get a clout that would send him reeling for three days. That set him off again, and you know, the funniest thing about this episode is that I was accompanying him because of a matter to do with a woman. That is why he had come to me. He needed support. A woman was way beyond his ken.'

She worked in Jogi's restaurant on the town side of Bodh Gaya. This was not the side Ahmed had crossed on his way to Thubten's tent. That had been the tourist side, which started soon after the half-desolate campus of Magadh University ended and a few large hotels appeared; beyond these, to the right, could be seen a massive outdoor statue of Buddha, towering over all the buildings. This relatively open side of Bodh Gaya spread around a main road with its temples in different national styles, curio shops and small restaurants with ambitious names, even a small public park. The road then ascended slightly and reached the Mahabodhi temple, the intricately carved seventh-century stone structure – now smothered with cement in a bid to 'restore' it – marking the spot where Siddhartha, the prince who left home to ponder about suffering, death and life, became the Buddha, the enlightened one, under the foliage of a tree. Then the road grew narrower and descended on the other side of the temple, where it finally split into two even narrower strands.

This was the native town side of Bodh Gaya. Behind it lay the mostly dry banks of the Phalgu river. This side had fewer and dingier shops; its restaurants had less ambitious names. Jogi's restaurant had no name; it was known by the name of its owner, who was a short, rotund man in his sixties. He was no mystic; Jogi was just what his parents had named him.

Jogi's restaurant – or Jogi's dhaba, as it was more often called – was a three-storey brick building, mostly unplastered. The upper storeys contained rooms that Jogi rented out, some for years, and some for a day or two. The ground floor contained rooms used by Jogi and his family, and a large hall, with a kitchen behind it. This hall was Jogi's dhaba, though the board propped outside, at the entrance, gave it no name. It just said in Hindi: food made of 'pure ghee' here.

The first time Ahmed went there, he was with a bunch of other guides. These were young men who hung around the shops and restaurants of Bodh Gaya, offering to exchange foreign currency or show you sights. Ahmed did not like going out with them – their talk was mostly of money, booze and women, and they often joked about taking advantage, monetary and sexual, of the tourists they had recently guided – but it was a close-knit band and Ahmed could not avoid them. He had known most of them from the time he used to stand in for Hanif Ustad, and he often tried his foreign languages on them – for many of these young men, mostly high school dropouts, spoke Thai or Japanese with greater fluency than they spoke English. Despite the years together, Ahmed remained wary of them, their physical jostling, their lewd jokes and the 'side businesses' – such as selling weed or procuring women – some of them also ran. On the other hand, they took to Ahmed with unexpected respect, seldom making him the target of their jokes.

They had been celebrating that evening. One of the guides was getting married the following week. 'Beginning of wife, end of life,' they told the prospective bridegroom, and dragged him to Jogi's dhaba for dinner. Ahmed was sitting with them, smoking over cups of tea in the square outside the Mahabodhi temple – for the season was dying and tourists were few – and could not refuse to go along.

Jogi knew all of them except Ahmed, who was elaborately introduced as the most brilliant of all guides and a great scholar from Phansa, and, for it proved his unproven greatness, a man who did not touch alcohol. After that, the men ordered beer – Jogi did not have a permit to sell alcohol but would procure it for reliable patrons – and a woman who had been working in the kitchen came over to get their order.

The men obviously knew her, and she knew them, for one of them said to her, after she had plunked metal plates down and taken their orders, 'Ah, what a ripe fruit.' The remark, though it made Ahmed flush and the other men smirk and nudge each other, was descriptive: there was something of the luscious fruit about this young woman, ruddily dark, with high cheekbones and slanted eyes, a tightness, a fullness, a ripeness that her sari could not hide. The woman was not flustered at all. 'Well beyond your reach, shorty,' she told the man. At which another of the men sang out, 'Fall into my hands, O ripe fruit.' The woman scoffed on her way back to the soot-blackened kitchen: 'You are not strong enough to hold me, twiggy.' All the men – except Ahmed, who was staring at his metal plate – laughed uproariously.

'Who is she?' he later asked one of the men. He was given a name, a Hindu one. But another man corrected the first one and gave another name, a Christian one this time. A third man offered a third name.

She was a woman of various names. One of them was Roshni.

The basic facts of Roshni's life were commonly known, and the men took turns narrating them to Ahmed, though in a hushed voice. She lived upstairs with her mother, who was said to be Muslim and was Jogi's keep. They used the English word 'keep'. The mother was ailing now and surely it was generous of Jogi to let her stay on, as she could not be of any further use to him, could she, and there had always been friction between her and Jogi's rightly wedded wife, who lived downstairs with him.

Then the girl was Jogi's natural daughter? No, the men laughed, do you see any resemblance? Everyone knows that Jogi keeps pestering her, but she won't let him dip his stick in her creek. Though it is not a creek that has remained unfished, the men laughed. Not by any means. She is said to have a penchant for the goras, but of course only if they pay her in dollars.

Whose daughter is she then? No one knows. Jogi half-pretends she is his daughter – so that he can keep her next to him, now that her mother is an old crone, good for nothing – but look at her, yaar, look at her when she comes by next time. There is nothing of Jogi in her. She is as dark as her mother, true, why I have never heard of a Muslim woman that dark, she looks like a Munda, but look at her legs, those sturdy calves, look at her cheekbones, those chinky eyes, don't you see it? Her father has to be a chink, probably one of those Tibetan monks who got a heatstroke meditating in April and went for her mother!

When Roshni – that is the name Ahmed decided he liked best – came back to their tables with the bill, scratched on a chit of paper, and as they debated who was paying what, the bridegroom being exempted on the condition that he would treat all of them after his wedding, Ahmed stole a bolder look at her, almost despite himself. She noticed it and smiled back at him. 'You are new,' she said. Then she added: 'I have seen you before in the square. You are always reading a book.' One of the men hastened to inform her that Ahmed was a great scholar from Phansa. She laughed as she counted their money. 'What is he doing with you empty-heads then?' was her parting shot as she flounced back.

Ahmed started going to Jogi's dhaba regularly. He had to eat somewhere on his days in Bodh Gaya. But he must have realized that pragmatism was not his only reason, for he never went there with any of the men.

I can imagine the relationship as it developed, though Devi's man had put it in only a few sparse words: 'In due course, Ahmed started helping Roshni with her homework, and with medicines and doctors for her mother.' It says everything one needs to know, but what one needs to know seems insufficient in such cases, doesn't it? Even a pragmatic businessman like me can do better: imagine … the clanking fan under which Ahmed sat as the year got warmer, Roshni just serving him first, maybe with a flirtatious joke that would leave him flustered and tongue-tied, then joining him at the table, despite Jogi shouting at her to get on with it, and slowly a conversation flowing between them – first a trickle blocked by the minutest of chores, then the many trickles uniting into a river that could sweep any interruption aside. I can imagine Ahmed's surprise when he realized Roshni was preparing for her Inter exams. He must have computed her age then and thought: Roshni might be just seventeen years old, but surely that is unlikely, for she could not have studied without many interruptions, and she must have lost at least a year or two in the process. I can see her bringing him some mathematical theorem or language problem, perhaps with a joke first – 'Say Mr Great Scholar, can you solve this?' – and then seeking more and more help from him. I can see Ahmed, naturally inclined to help others, offering to fetch a doctor when her mother had one of her collapses … I can imagine all this spread over the next year or two, though, as I have already confessed to you, this ability to imagine large segments of Ahmed's life leaves me shaken too. I ask myself: did you always have this hidden ability to speak about things that you have not witnessed, not *seen*, or has it been bestowed, a gift or a curse, on you by the very events driving you, here and now, to confess to a stranger?

Around the same time, the report specified, Ahmed had his falling out with the religious Muslims of his mohalla. This had to do with Shab-e-baraat.

As I had learnt from Ahmed, there is a tradition in many Muslim families to visit the graves of the dear departed, clean them, light incense sticks and pray at the graves during Shab-e-baraat. Ahmed had been accompanying Ammajaan to his father's grave year after year. That year, mother and son got ready as usual – each took a longer bath and put on fresh clothes, Ammajaan fumbled in her rusting Godrej almirah for the box of incense sticks she kept there – and set out on a rickshaw for the graveyard, which was a couple of kilometres from their house. They had greater reason this year to look forward to this annual ritual, as the graveyard had been finally enclosed in a boundary wall under a new management. It had been modernized, it was said. Ahmed had been there once after the changes were made, the wall built, and he had come back and given an enthused report to Ammajaan, who was now too old and infirm to go to the graveyard more than once a year. 'The walls prevent goats and dogs from entering, and there is even a gateman to keep loiterers out! Taps have been installed at regular intervals to wash feet and hands, Ammajaan, and to water the flower plants and pomegranate bushes at the graves. Garbage has been cleared away, paths laid out. The new management is finally doing some managing!' Ahmed had told Ammajaan.

As their rickshaw pulled up at the gate of the graveyard, Ammajaan pushed aside her face cover – with age she permitted herself some leeway with the purdah – and said in appreciation of the developments, 'Subhaan-Allah. Bahut accha kaam kiya hai management ne! Dil khush kar diya!' Do you understand that? No? Well, it means: God be praised. The management has done excellent work. It pleases the heart.

Then she waited for Ahmed to get off the rickshaw and come around to her side to help her alight and hand her the walking stick she needed. All this took some time. The sun was shining. Sparrows were fluttering on the wall next to the gate.

Ahmed helped Ammajaan to the gate, which was slightly ajar, but just as he held it open for her, the gateman came running. He had been sitting at a nearby kiosk. He knew both Ammajaan and Ahmed. 'Ahmed sahab,' he shouted from a distance as he ran towards them, 'Khalajaan cannot go in.'

The sparrows took off with a whirr, like that of pages turned by the wind.

Both Ammajaan and Ahmed were surprised. 'Why not, mian?' asked Ammajaan, a trifle brusquely.

'Manahi hai,' said the gatekeeper. 'Women cannot enter the graveyard, Khalajaan.'

'What errant nonsense,' replied Ammajaan. 'I have been entering it every year for longer than you have lived on this earth!'

'It was wrong. It has been prohibited.' The gateman was obdurate.

An argument unfolded, with Ahmed pitching in to support his mother, and a crowd gathering. Two management committee members also came up. One of them had worked with Ahmed's father, before quitting and getting a job in Saudi Arabia; he had retired and returned home only a couple of years ago. He was clear about it: 'Women are too weak, too soft-hearted to enter graveyards. They cannot bear it. It is for their good that they are prohibited from entering.'

'It has been confirmed by reliable sources that the subject was not a man to get angry,' the report put it in Devi's register. 'But that day he got excessively angry. This surprised the crowd, which had been neutral until then, it was recalled by three of the witnesses interviewed.' I wondered if Ahmed's anger was provoked by the new rule or by the fact that no one in the crowd supported him.

'Witness Number 3, also quoted above, recalls the culmination of the episode in these words, translated verbatim: You do not just start shouting at a Haji, telling him, a member of two mosque and one graveyard committees, what the Holy Quran says, do you? The old gentleman had worked with his father too. And the Haji, he is dead now, Allah bestow peace on him, honoured that association; he kept addressing Ahmed's Ammajaan as bhabhi, which is the proper way. But Ahmed? He was stubborn, quoting from this and quoting from that, as if he was a sheikh, not a lowly guide who everyone in the mohalla knew ate with Tibetans and in Hindu hotels. We did not like Ahmed's attitude that day. No, I did not. He had become too big for his boots, having earned easy money and been with unbelievers too often and too long. There was some mumbling. The hotheads in the crowd would have roughed him up had his Ammajaan not been there. And it was his Ammajaan who pulled him away, literally by his sleeve. Let's go, son, she said. Let's return home. The day will be over soon and there are things to do.'

The elder who had worked with Ahmed's father was very proper. He apologized for hurting bhabhi's feelings, and said to Ahmed, 'Son, you can go in.'

'Not without Ammajaan,' Ahmed replied. It was known that he never entered the graveyard again, except once. This too turned many of the mohalla people against him, and perhaps led to the problems he had over the matter of Roshni later on.

I was reading this part of the report late in the night, sitting at the dining table. It was after midnight. Even the servants were sleeping. The house and the streets outside were quiet, except for the occasional car and a faint yapping of street dogs from different directions.

I had woken up to read the report. I had not been able to fall fast asleep, my mind returning to it in sleep, with that dream of the hand clutching at a sleeve recurring. It had returned three or four times that night, and finally my half-awake mind had identified a new element: I had recognized the hand clutching at what I had thought until then was my sleeve. It was not an unknown hand, not the ancient mariner's. It was not even Ahmed's hand, as you might have assumed. It was my hand – I had recognized the scar that I have carried from the time I fell down and cut myself while doing the hurdles in school. It was *my* hand. And the sleeve? I just could not tell whose sleeve it was!

That had chased all sleep from my eyes. At first, I had lain there, spread-eagled, staring up blankly at the ceiling. Then I had stolen out of bed – my wife is a sound sleeper – and returned to reading the report on the dining table.

Now I put it aside because a memory had returned to me. It was from some years ago. Some of the staff, including Ahmed, were taking a tea break. The office has a nook with tea and coffee machines and a few chairs. Once in a while, when staff members take a break, I join them too – it serves to add the human touch to the business and also ensure that the pauses are not too long. It was one of those occasions.

When I joined them that day, they were talking about the old tragedy queens and kings of cinema, discussing who was better – Guru Dutt, Dilip Kumar, Meena Kumari, Nargis, Rekha – at playing tragic roles. They were discussing the great tragic scenes. Ahmed was there too, listening but not saying much, which was his usual way, unless asked.

One of the men turned to him. 'Ahmed, you have not told us what is the most tragic scene in your view.'

Ahmed had said, almost instantly, as if it burst out from deep within him, as if it was a scene framed forever in his heart, seared into his mind: 'An old woman hobbling on a stick along half a kilometre of a railway track, a hazardous, shit-infested track, to catch one last glimpse of her husband's grave.'

'What film was it?' the colleague asked.

'It wasn't a film,' Ahmed replied, and withdrew from the company, back into his own cubicle.

Can't you imagine it? It might have happened the same day or some days later.

I see it this way. Ammajaan and Ahmed return to

their section of the house. Ahmed is angry; Ammajaan is silent. They go through the other rituals of Shab-e-baraat; they eat the maida ka halwa. But Ammajaan is unusually silent. Then she says, perhaps only to herself, but aloud, 'If only I could have seen him once more.'

Attentive Ahmed, now preternaturally sensitive to his mother's mood, overhears and enquires immediately, 'Seen whom?'

'Your father's grave,' Ammajaan replies.

Ahmed is immediately ready to go out and argue with the graveyard management committee again. But Ammajaan does not want that. She forbids it. Instead, she suggests they could walk along the railway tracks behind the graveyard; she knows from previous visits that her husband's grave is on that side and would be visible from the railway tracks.

Can you imagine it? The old woman, unstable, balancing herself on the tracks and between them, the tracks that contain so much disposed from the trains, the tracks that are used by poorer Indians to defecate, the tracks that can, at any moment, bring a train rushing at her. And her son, supporting her, keeping an ear open for the slightest sound of an approaching engine, restraining himself from hurrying her and still wanting her to move as fast as she can … And then they reach the spot, and she identifies the grave from a distance, cups her hands and offers the usual prayer. Then they turn back and return the way they had come.

It made sense now, what Ahmed had said then in my office: 'An old woman hobbling on a stick along half a kilometre of a railway track, a hazardous, shit-infested track, to catch one last glimpse of her husband's grave.'

You might think I have forgotten about that walk with Thubten, that my story has gone off in other directions, become involved in an intricate past. But that is not the case. Because, you see, that day when Ahmed asked his Tibetan friend Thubten to accompany him, he had made up his mind. He was going to ask Roshni to marry him.

He had known her for three years now, during which she had finished her Inter, with second-class marks. Two months back Roshni's mother had died. A few weeks ago, Roshni had complained to Ahmed that Jogi had tried to come into her room one night, drunk, and after she had physically thrown him out, he had given her notice to vacate. She had asked Ahmed to help her find 'safe lodgings', but Ahmed had other ideas. He could have asked her himself, but of course he wouldn't.

'Imagine Ahmed asking a woman to marry him?' Thubten told Devi's man. 'It is so damn funny! No, he wanted me to ask her on his behalf. Matchmaker, matchmaker, find me a match! I think he would have wanted his mother or some old woman to do the job, but that was not possible. And tell you what, it fucking worked: I was a bloody good matchmaker. I don't want to take too much credit though: it had been clear to everyone for months that the girl was totally in love with Ahmed. Clear to everyone except Ahmed, that is!'

Devi's Phansa report had fewer details about what happened next, except that Ahmed and Roshni were married by a mullah in Bodh Gaya, and Ammajaan accepted it. Not everyone else did though, as I think I have told you. Some mohalla people wanted Roshni to be converted to Islam and the niqaah to be performed again. They did not believe Ahmed's claim that Roshni was a Muslim. 'She doesn't look like a Muslim,' said those who did not know anything about her. And those who had heard about her from Bodh Gaya said, 'Who knows what her father was?'

But Ahmed refused, and – what disappointed the deeply religious in particular – Ammajaan defended him. 'How can a Muslim be converted again to Islam?'

she maintained stubbornly. It isolated Ahmed from many in the mohalla, but he did not seem to care. His world was his mother and now Roshni, who imitated her mother-in-law's dress codes despite Ahmed's objections.

'They will never accept you no matter what you do,' he told her.

'Do you think that is why I am doing this?' she answered him. Then she added: 'I only want to be seen by you.'

6

Devi's second report – the report on Ahmed and Roshni's years in Mumbai and Surat – must have reached him around the same time the Missus told me she had asked Shuja Shirmali over to dinner, because three or four days before the dinner I received a phone call from Devi. Once again my discussion with Devi changed my questions. Ahmed's realities, it appeared, shifted with every new enquiry into it, as if he was not a solid human being but something amorphous, imaginary, ghostly.

I was in my car, being driven to office when the mobile buzzed.

Devi's opening words took me by surprise. 'Are you alone?' he asked. I told him I was on my way to work.

'Boss, can you come to see me today? The other report has arrived.'

'Why don't you just send it over by courier, marked confidential like last time? That way I will have it sooner.'

I could sense Devi hesitating. Then he replied, in a lower tone, 'I can, but. It is just that not all the information is there in the written report. I can give you a verbal summary.'

I was surprised. 'Why isn't all the information in the report, Devi?' I asked.

There was a moment of silence on the other end. Then Devi chuckled. 'My innocent friend,' he replied, 'as governments tend to put it, some of it is sensitive.'

'Sensitive?'

'Or classified. It cannot be written down.'

As I was not too busy that day, I arranged with Devi to see him immediately, and asked the driver to take me to his office instead of mine.

It was only when Devi shut the door to his office and locked it that I noticed something I had not really heeded on my previous visits. His walls and door were padded. What I had seen as a kind of 1970s decor – the sort found in some Delhi and Kolkata restaurants in particular – was insulation and padding meant to make the room soundproof. Once the door was closed and the shutters pulled, I could not hear a sound from the outside, and obviously no one outside could hear us.

Devi returned to his plush revolving chair and sank into it. He noticed me looking around. 'Part of the business,' he explained.

'You make me nervous,' I said, and I partly meant it, even as the other part of me felt amused at this cloak-and-dagger scenario.

'Mostly for show, boss. But sometimes we do work for people who want more secrecy than you do, my friend, and they have enemies who can be hugely curious,' he replied. 'This time it is best to be careful in your case, too.'

I laughed. 'What can be so hush-hush about Ahmed's days in Mumbai?' I asked, even though old fears were again surfacing in my mind. Mumbai has a huge underworld; it is known to have terrorist links. Was Ahmed involved in stuff like that, after all?

'It is not really his days in Mumbai. It is the way they ended.'

Here is the story he told me, minus the interruptions I made and the innuendoes Devi employed.

Roshni and Ahmed left for Mumbai within a week of Ammajaan's death 'from old-age-related complications', as the death certificate put it. She was buried next to her husband, and Ahmed entered the graveyard for the last time. But after the body had been laid down, Ahmed scandalized the gathering once again by not saying the required prayer by the graveside. Instead, he left immediately; he was seen walking out of the graveyard and up the railway tracks behind it. Then he stood at the point closest to the grave, on the railway tracks, covered his head with a handkerchief and said the prayer for the departed.

With Ammajaan buried, what reason could Roshni and Ahmed have had to stay on? There was nothing connecting them to that community any more, as Ahmed's gesture indicated. And they appear to have settled into Mumbai quite easily. That huge city which has accepted so many strangers also embraced them.

Ahmed had used one of his contacts – a rich businessman from Mumbai, whose family and friends he had guided around Bodh Gaya and Nalanda on different occasions – to get a job. This said a lot to me. Devi's man could not know it, and hence Devi's narration did not mention how unusual it was for Ahmed to make such a request. I had seen Ahmed working in our office for years, and he never asked anyone for anything if he could do it himself. You know how one asks a colleague to pass a pencil or a sharpener? Can you pass me this? Will you toss me that? Ahmed never did so. He would get up and fetch things himself, no matter how minor, moving in his usual unhurried manner. So, the fact that he asked someone for a favour – a job – indicated to me the intensity of Ahmed's desire to leave his mohalla.

The businessman might have initially thought he was doing Ahmed a favour, but he was astute enough to realize Ahmed's potential: within two years, he had moved Ahmed from being a warehouse supervisor to a more responsible desk in his main office. And then, in 2001, he made Ahmed the in-charge of their Surat office.

Devi covered Roshni and Ahmed's years in Mumbai in a few prosaic lines, reserving the bulk of his words to describe how they ended. 'They were happy, I suppose,' he told me. 'They rented a flat in the suburbs, and Ahmed commuted about two hours every day to work. They were liked by their neighbours, and participated in neighbourhood activities and festivities: you know, the usual movie show or puja. It was a mixed neighbourhood, mostly Hindus, but also a smattering of Muslims, Christians, Sikhs, one or two elderly and impoverished Parsis. Roshni still observed purdah, but less rigorously, going out in public with her face uncovered, participating in neighbourhood gatherings without Ahmed, sometimes even going to the cinema with the two or three female friends she had made. Ahmed and Roshni often went out during vacations and weekends, either to the cinema or to one of the beaches. Nothing to distinguish them from a thousand other newlyweds.'

Isn't it sad how easily we skim over happiness? I have done it all my life too, inadvertently, ignorantly. It is only now I realize, dimly, that I have been doing so for years. I recall entering the girls' room sometimes at night, just to check if they are sleeping, and observing their blanket-covered forms lightly breathing. The soft heave and fall of the sheets in that room of toys and posters. A feeling of calm and joy washes over me, but I do not tarry to savour it; I rush back to whatever worry or nonsense or TV show engages my attention downstairs. I think of my wife talking about some vacuous literary event – banter over a cosy family dinner – and how, instead of appreciating the simple moment, I try to contain my irritation at the missus going on and on about something that does not interest me at all. What did Ahmed say once, during one of those office discussions? Yes, this was it, an Ahmedism if ever there was one: 'One need not search for happiness; one needs to stop for it.'

It is only now that I am beginning to understand what he meant by it. We skip happiness, as Devi's report did, we don't pause for it. The report had nothing to say of Roshni and Ahmed walking the sands of Juhu Beach, eating bhelpuri out of the same paper plate, the breeze blowing Roshni's face cover over her head, as if it was a cloud following her. The report had nothing to say of Roshni riding pillion on the motorcycle Ahmed had bought, either to go shopping or to the cinema. The report had nothing to say of the two sitting next to each other, watching the rich and handsome hero and the accomplished and beautiful heroine singing out their larger-than-life-happiness across a dozen locales on three continents, and feeling not the slightest trace of envy, for Roshni's hand has slipped into Ahmed's in the darkness of the theatre and this little space between them is more than all the continents can offer.

Happiness! Who has time for happiness? Definitely not people like Devi – and me.

I interrupted Devi's narrative. 'Did they join any society?' I asked him, 'Ahmed, especially.'

'Society, boss?' he asked, surprised.

'I mean' – and I felt embarrassed to spell it out – 'is there any indication that Ahmed might have had Islamist sympathies or met people like that?'

'No, nothing. Quite the contrary: he does not seem to have gone to the mosque any longer, and only turned up for the open-air Eid prayers.'

I was relieved. Despite the suspicions I had harboured soon after the evening in Ahmed's flat – suspicions that, I confess, did return to me occasionally – there was little to associate Ahmed with fundamentalist Islam. True, he did not drink alcohol, but then he did not seem to insist on halal meat either; he ate the meat served to him during parties and restaurant outings, and he allowed the tilak mark to be put on his forehead when we held the usual, rather perfunctory, puja in the office. And yet, it was difficult to slot him – yes, I think that was the root of all these suspicions that returned to me despite my better self. That is why I had to ask Devi the question.

Take, for instance, this episode from Ahmed's fifth year with me, or maybe the sixth. By then the business had expanded. We had just moved into bigger premises, the one we occupy now. In tandem with all these developments, I had decided to issue company credit cards to my top four employees, and of course Ahmed was one of them. These were people who took clients and partners out for lunches and so on, when I was too busy to do so or the guests were not big enough for me to bother with; it would be simpler for them to put cheques directly on the company account, instead of filling forms to get a reimbursement.

But Ahmed, I was informed by the accountant, had refused to accept the credit card. He had said he did not use credit cards. He used only debit cards or paid with cash.

Of course, I had to take this up with Ahmed on the first opportunity. And I did. I asked him, as soon as I found him alone, 'I am told you do not use credit cards, Ahmed?'

'I have never had one, Mehrotra sa'ab. I would prefer not to.'

'Why? Is it for religious reasons?' (Even I was aware of Islamic banking and the reputed objection that religious Muslims have to charging or paying interest.)

'Not really, Mehrotra sa'ab. But who can stand security for the future? One either has debt, or one has time.'

'That is Greek to me, Ahmed. And Sanskrit too,' I had said, laughing. 'Can't you put it in plain English or Hindi?'

He had thought for a second and then said, 'Debt

is a slap in the face of time. I don't have debts; I have all time.'

It had made even less sense to me, but I had pointed out the obvious: 'All money is debt today, Ahmed.'

'You can make your own money, Mehrotra sa'ab.'

'It is called forgery, Ahmed,' I had joked.

'Not that kind of money!' and he had uttered the grunt that passed for a laugh with him.

But now Devi was leaning closer to me, across the desk, and his voice had become a loud whisper. His look had changed, turned wary and secretive, and it accentuated his heavy jowls, which he hid behind the goatee, and the deeply furrowed brows he usually lightened with his standard jovial demeanour. He was obviously back in his cloak-and-dagger mode.

'Do you remember 2002?' he asked me.

'2002? Let me see. Wasn't that the golden jubilee of Queen Elizabeth? Did the Iraq war begin then?'

'No, no, think of Mumbai, of Surat.'

'Mumbai?' I shrugged. 'Nothing comes to mind.'

'The Gujarat riots,' Devi said.

'Ah! That was the year?'

'That was the year.'

'It affected Surat, didn't it?' I asked, a horrific suspicion crossing my mind.

'Yes, it did,' Devi looked grim, 'Roshni and Ahmed had just moved into a new flat in a part of the city a few months ago.'

Then he handed me some sheets, obviously from the report that he did not want me to have in its entirety. 'Read these,' he said. 'My man does not want me to include this in any report to be given out officially – to you or anyone else. I can understand why. We are businessmen, boss – professionals, not activists.'

It began many kilometres away from Ahmed and Roshni's beloved Mumbai, which they must have been reluctant to leave for Surat. Why did they leave? Ahmed might have been ambitious in those days, or he might just have been too polite to refuse a promotion by his benefactor and employer. Or, perhaps, they had missed living in a smaller town – and Surat is a relatively small place in Gujarat.

A train was set on fire in Godhra on 27 February 2002, and the fire spread across Gujarat.

Violence, Ahmed had once said, is a virus; it spreads by contaminating others. Ahmed had been trying to defend Gandhi's philosophy of ahimsa, which was being criticized by a couple of his colleagues who claimed to support the Hindutva ideology of the BJP for intellectual and not religious reasons. That is when he had said these words. I think his point was that the only way to resist violence is to refuse to harbour it, or you become a carrier of the virus and it spreads further through you. But what if the virus is injected into you? What if the doctors of your society infect you with the virus?

You might look bewildered, and, to be honest, I had to dredge up the facts of the Gujarat riots on Wikipedia too, so deep down in the swamp of my consciousness had the tragedy sunk. It was not something that was discussed much in my circles, except when some major accusation surfaced in the newspapers, and even then, fleetingly. It did not belong to my world. I know that now.

The sheets from Devi's report kept the information to bare facts, always carefully attributed to public sources. It had started neither in Mumbai nor in Surat. A trainload of Hindutva activists, returning from the site of a mosque in Ayodhya, destroyed by Hindu fanatics some years ago because it was said to have been built on the site of a temple marking the birthplace of Lord Rama. Do you know of it? You must. Well, then, this train was set on fire. Muslims were accused of doing it, though later investigation suggests it may have been an accident. More than fifty Hindu pilgrims died in the fire. The fire spread to various towns and cities of Gujarat, then governed by our new and great prime minister.

As I said, the sheets I read in Devi's office, after which he took them from me and put them through the shredder on a side cabinet, were taciturn about the details. This is all they said, as far as I can recall, about the main tragedy: 'Based entirely on what the newspapers reported (see Appendix 3A) and not any evidence obtained or sought by this investigator, the riots that followed led to the death of 790 Muslims – some put the estimate at double that number – and 254 Hindus. Thousands were injured and rendered homeless. It was reported in national newspapers (see Appendix 3B) that women were raped and impaled on spears; children were burned alive. The government of Gujarat was accused – and later absolved, it has to be noted – of purposefully dragging its feet, to give vigilante Hindutva groups, some supposedly led by politicians, a chance to teach 'those Muslims a lesson' (see Appendix 3C).'

Roshni, as Devi told me, was one of those Muslims.

But the sheets said more about what happened to Roshni and Ahmed. I suppose they had to; after all, Devi's people were known to do a thorough job. And I think that is why they had to be shredded.

The fire came to Ahmed's part of Surat when he was not there. He had gone to work. Roshni was alone in their small flat.

At office, when Ahmed heard of riots in town, he was not overly worried. They had settled in well, and by now Roshni knew many of the neighbours. Ahmed trusted them. He was confident the neighbours would not harm Roshni.

It was not the neighbours who harmed Roshni. A mob came into the neighbourhood from outside, led by minor politicians of the ruling party. It had a municipal list of houses belonging to Muslims, and another list of flats rented by Muslims.

The mob went about its task methodically. In that sense, it was surely not a mob. When it banged on Roshni's door, she did not open it. They broke it down. Then they dragged Roshni out of the flat. Only one neighbour tried to protect her. (I would like to believe this was so because all the men, like Ahmed, were away, stuck in the places where they worked.) It was an old South Indian man, who tried to tell the crowd that Roshni and her husband were part of their community, that they were not 'bad' Muslims, that they even participated in neighbourhood pujas. The leaders of the mob were in no mood to listen. They had not been able to catch many Muslims; most of the others in this locality seemed to have fled. They needed to kill.

When the old man continued to protest, he was shoved aside by one of the leaders, and cuffed and kicked back into his flat by other men. There he was restrained by the frightened women of his household.

It was this organized mob that dragged Roshni down the stairs. They ripped the veil off her. They mocked her. 'Where is your God?' they shouted. 'Where is your bastard man?' they mocked. 'No one can save you now, you Pakistani whore!'

Roshni, the neighbours reported, said nothing. She just sat in the dust, head bowed, as if lost in deep thought. She did not even react when the South Indian man, in one last attempt to help her, screamed that she was not Muslim. 'Look at her,' he shouted, from his doorway, where the women held him back, 'Look at her. Does she look Muslim?' But Roshni did not ply this sliver of doubt inserted in the mob by the old man. She did not claim she was not Muslim. She did not say anything. She neither cried nor remonstrated; she never pleaded.

In that description, I see her as I now see Ahmed: people with deep and mysterious sources of strength and calm, men and women of a kind we fail to recognize in the crowd, because we no longer pause to look, for we associate strength with violence, or at least with action. Was that why, when I had looked back into the hall of the literary party on the evening of my fateful encounter with the invisible halwa – the party my wife had dragged me to, the one thrown to honour an award-winning 'son of the nation' on his second trip to India – I had failed to find anyone resembling Ahmed in that crowd of movers and shakers?

Roshni's calm frustrated the mob. They were men on the move in a nation on the move, and all she did was sit immobile on the ground, her head bowed, neither defiant nor submissive. Would weeping and pleading have saved her? Should she have grabbed the feet of the men, supplicated them in the name of their gods or hers? Should she have abased herself, done violence to her own self, torn out her hair, slapped her cheeks, beat her head, before they could do violence to her, and thus appeased their blind craving for action, for change and movement?

Who knows?

It was one of the leaders of the mob – easy to identify but never arrested, of course – who poured kerosene on her bowed head. The crowd around her withdrew, as the sweet smell of the fuel spread. They were ordinary people: they knew the smell from domestic situations. Suddenly a space opened up around her. She was there in that space, with the leader next to her. Then the leader took a step back. And then another. He struck a match and threw it on Roshni.

Some in the mob erupted into shouts of glory to the divine nation. Some started walking away in silence.

I cannot imagine it any more. Or I can only imagine it as its opposite: a stone thrown into a lake, how the stone sinks, and the ripples spread, and then there is nothing.

Then – in *my* world – there is nothing.

When Devi finished narrating Roshni's fate, there was at least a minute of silence in his padded room. I did not know what to say.

Then I said, 'So, Ahmed's wife is dead?'

Devi nodded.

'There is no chance she might have survived, perhaps badly disfigured?' I asked.

'No, boss,' replied Devi. 'Ahmed claimed and buried her charred remains in a Muslim graveyard, three or four days later, when such things could be done.'

You do realize that knowledge of Roshni's fate did not make matters any easier for me? If, on the one hand, it left me with no choice but to face up to Ahmed's basic insanity – his traumatized refusal to accept the death of his wife – on the other hand, it added to the sympathy and affection I felt for that quiet, peaceful, almost entirely self-contained man. I could not even blame him for refusing to accept the death of a woman he had obviously adored.

But could I ignore his madness? Did I not owe honesty to him – and to myself and my business? Was I not responsible for the others who worked for me – and with him?

I was still turning these issues over in my mind when the Friday dinner with Shuja Shirmali finally came around. My questions had changed yet again, but of course I did still have questions for the Muslim novelist.

Shuja Shirmali was in his sixties, a large man with a short, bristly beard. He had a deep voice, tailored for audiences, and an appropriate couplet – Zauq, Ghalib, Faiz, Iqbal – for every topic of conversation. The missus and the two younger writers she had invited for company lapped up his every word.

Even I, despite a degree of scepticism (he made

Islam sound like it was Dalai Lama's Buddhism minus the idols), was entertained and almost distracted from my obsession with Ahmed.

But I did manage to insert a question unobtrusively into the conversation, just before dessert was served. It was gajar ka halwa, the only kind of halwa we make at home.

You see, all my questions had finally boiled down to this one, and its answer, I was convinced, would help me do the right thing in office. I felt the proper thing to do, as far as my business and other employees were concerned, was to let Ahmed go. But I still hesitated, for I did not want to be unfair to him as a Muslim. What did I know? Perhaps belief in cohabiting with ghosts was a feature of Islamic beliefs?

But Shuja was conclusive about it, when I asked him. 'There are really no ghosts in Islam. Souls, yes, but they do not wander about on earth like ghosts. Of course, many Muslims believe in ghosts, but that is all local beliefs. In Islam, Allah placed only two kinds of reasoning beings on earth: human kind, made of earth, and the djinns, made of fire. There is no rationale in Islamic thinking to explain ghosts, though I quite like the idea. Spiritual power, as in some saints, at least we Sufis believe in – but that is not a matter of ghosts. The Sufi saints do not walk the earth as ghosts, they simply have the spiritual power – accorded to them by Allah – to intercede with Allah on behalf of ordinary human beings. There are actually no ghosts in Islam. It might well be the only religion in the world without ghosts!'

Everything was unresolved. All those reports, all that thought, and nothing was a jot clearer. All the explanations seemed wrong. But what I could not avoid facing was the fact of Ahmed's discrepant behaviour: he pretended that his dead wife was alive. What was more, after years of this private pretence, for some reason his fictional world had spilled into our factual one. He had inserted me into the fiction of his wife the evening he offered me that plate of nimkis and the invisible halwa.

Facts have to be faced. I have strongly believed this. And whatever the fiction behind Ahmed's existence, the fact was this: he was living a fiction, and that fiction was gradually living him. He was not reliable. There was no avoiding the matter: he had to be relieved of his responsibilities in my business. I had to protect myself and the others.

Now I knew that in believing his dead wife was still cohabiting with him, he was not even being very Muslim. That knowledge lifted a burden from my soul.

It would not be unfair to act as I should: even his religion did not permit belief in ghosts.

It still took me all weekend to gird myself up to the endeavour. I had to face Ahmed. There was nothing else to do.

On Monday, I called him into my office. And I told him, point-blank: 'Ahmed, I have the highest regard for what you have done for us in all these years. But businesses change, and I am going to begin a process of restructuring. This will involve some transfers and layoffs. I am afraid we will have to let you go soon.'

If Ahmed was surprised, he hid it well.

'Is it something I have done wrong?' he enquired passively.

'No, not at all.'

He gave me his faint, slightly sad smile. 'Mehrotra sa'ab, you know you can be honest with me.'

'Nothing to do with your work in any case, Ahmed,' I replied. 'We need to restructure, as I said.'

'Ah,' replied Ahmed, 'it was that evening at my flat. I had told Roshni the halwa wasn't something for you, but she insisted …'

'There was no halwa, Ahmed,' I broke in, a bit angrily.

'But there was, Mehrotra sa'ab, my wife had made it …'

'Your wife died, Ahmed. She was murdered,' I broke in again, this time with genuine sorrow in my voice, I would hope. 'I was sorry to learn of it, and I wish such saffron ruffians are brought to book. Lock them up and throw away the key, I say. But, you have to face it, Ahmed, your wife is no longer with you.'

Ahmed sat in the chair, his smile still fixed on his face, looking down into his lap. The sudden silence in the room made me hear all kinds of noises: the air conditioner, people talking outside, a phone ringing. Then he muttered something I couldn't hear.

'Beg your pardon,' I said.

'Roshni is always with me, Mehrotra sa'ab,' he repeated, a bit louder.

I took a risk. After all, I was convinced I was dealing with a deeply disturbed man. I stood up, went around the desk and put one hand on Ahmed's shoulder.

'You are a rational man, Ahmed, a practical person. You need to face up to it,' I said.

He looked up in surprise. 'But I have always faced up to it.' There was something chilling about the calm and stubborn manner in which he responded. I felt repulsed, almost threatened. I struggled to keep my voice even.

'This won't do, Ahmed,' I said, returning to my chair. 'It is bad for you, it is bad for business. I am giving you one year's leave, fully paid. If you see an expert and come back in a state that I feel is good for you, you can ask to have your job back. Otherwise, well, you have a year's paid leave to find something else.'

Ahmed thought about it. 'I won't need more than a year,' he said, as if to himself. 'No, I don't think it will last more than a year now.'

'I am glad you agree, Ahmed,' I replied. 'You need help.'

Ahmed smiled again, this time more broadly than he usually did.

At that moment, his very assurance and smile revealed him as irrevocably demented to me, and one part of me finally wrote him off as a reasonable person. Had he raved or argued, had he revealed a nervous tic or a shaking hand, I would have hoped for him, as one hopes for a suffering fellow being. Had he even been angry at me – after all, I was a Hindu! – I told myself I would have reached out and grasped the hands of the man who had buried his beloved as a heap of charred bones and blackened flesh. I told myself I would have shared his tears. But this? Can one pity suffering that refuses to show? Can one comfort someone who remains calm? Can one hope for the healing of a patient who refuses to acknowledge the chasm between health and illness, sanity and madness? Answer me those questions, before you judge me!

'Thank you for your generosity, Mehrotra sa'ab,' Ahmed said, smiling, and moved towards the door. Then he turned and added: 'I have all the help I need.'

He closed the door softly behind him, and I discovered that, despite the air-conditioning, my forehead was beaded in sweat, my heart thumping so hard that I thought everyone could hear it.

7

Roughly a year must have passed. I had stopped thinking of Ahmed: he never contacted me after clearing out his cubicle. Oh no, he did once, indirectly: we had given him a farewell gift, a new laptop. A week after he left, he sent us a thank you card. The staff pinned it up in the coffee nook, and it is probably still hanging there, though, to be honest, I no longer join the others during coffee or tea breaks. But that was it: just that card. Nothing more, and honestly, I was relieved.

Do not misread me. I am not a stone-hearted man. But I try to live a sensible, useful life, and what Ahmed had done by presenting me with that non-existent plate of halwa was, what can I say, it was deeply disturbing, if not totally inconsiderate as well. The half-explanation he had given was not much help either. Could I absolve him of madness or serious psychological troubles by beginning to believe in ghosts – and a halwa I could not even see? Though I felt for Ahmed and had many fond memories of our years together, building up the business brick by brick, rationally, systematically, when I thought of the plate, I was filled with repugnance, resentment, yes, even rancour against him. Why did he have to plunge me into his delusions and problems? And our last interview, the way he left, calm and smiling, demented beyond redemption, with his total refusal to acknowledge the world of sense and caring?

As the months passed, my dream of the familiar hand clutching an unknown sleeve stopped recurring. I started sleeping soundly. It was back to business as usual.

I thought less and less of Ahmed, and that day, when his name came up, I was almost surprised to hear it. I had not thought of Ahmed at all for weeks, maybe months, before that. His name popped up because the sub-accountant, a young man who had been appointed only six months ago, walked into my office with a ledger and enquired, 'Sir, this Mr

Ahmed, who has been given his full salary in absence for a year – his year comes to an end next month. I suppose we should instruct the bank to stop paying him, shouldn't we?'

'Has it been a year?' I asked.

'It will be after next month.'

'Well, then, unless we hear from him, in which case I am to be consulted before any action is taken, instruct the bank to stop making the payments after next month,' I said almost unthinkingly, like reading out from a book. And I was pleased with the fact that the recurrence of Ahmed's name did not seem to cause me any ghostly agitation. I had distanced that evening from my life. I was behaving as I should: like a sensible businessman.

It must have been a day or two after this episode that I returned to office from a lunch meeting with some visiting businessmen, and found something wrapped in a clean white towel lying on my desk. I was surprised. I unknotted the towel and its folds revealed a steel tiffin box – exactly like the one Ahmed used to bring with him. A bit smaller though, containing only two compartments: a small top one and a deeper bottom one. A delicious smell was emanating from it. There was cinnamon in that fragrance, and cardamom, and half a dozen other minute herbs and seeds I could not identify for they grow on an earth I have seldom stopped to observe.

The smell had a physical presence. It swirled out of the tiffin box and filled the room in waves. It evoked a strange feeling of longing and peace in me, and I could feel my mouth water. In the light of what happened, I have thought of this moment again and again, and I assure you, what I felt at that moment was peace and longing – not the longing of unrequited desire but a longing that came with a feeling of trust in its fulfilment. Had I felt terror then, or even doubt, I would have understood it better.

So there I stood, on the side of my desk where I seat visitors. The towel – white cotton – lay unfolded on my desk. In the middle of it sat the tiffin carrier that reminded me, once again in two days, of Ahmed, who had been gone for almost a year.

I opened the first compartment. It contained nimkis, exactly like those Ahmed had served me in his flat. I took it off and put it aside. The deeper bottom compartment contained halwa: it was of a consistency much denser than a dip but not solid; its colour was that of rain clouds in monsoon, a dark, pregnant grey. The fragrance filling my office came from the halwa.

I took a nimki, dunked it in the halwa and popped

it into my mouth. It was delicious. It was heavenly! I ate a bit more. Then I looked around for a note. There was none.

I tapped the buzzer to call my peon. 'Who brought this?' I asked him. He looked at the tiffin carrier and shrugged. 'Must have been during my lunch break, sahab,' he said.

'Don't you lock my door when you go?' I reprimanded him.

'I always do, sahab,' he pleaded.

I did not retort that he was contradicting himself. He had not been appointed for his capacity to think clearly. That was not his job. I waved him away, sat down in one of the visitor's chairs and ate a bit more nimki and halwa. There was enough for three or four people. I was sure the missus would love it. She loves these Muslim dishes in any case, and, honestly, this was the best halwa I had ever eaten.

Then a thought struck me. I called back the peon and asked him if any of our Muslim employees was working today. We had only two, after Ahmed had left. The peon said they were not.

'Why not?' I asked him.

'They are on leave today,' he replied.

'Why?'

'They have a festival, sahab.'

'Shab-e-baraat?'

'Yes, sahab, I think that is what it is called, sahab.'

He looked relieved. I dismissed him again. Then – as I said I am not an insensitive person – I started feeling guilty about Ahmed. I did not regret letting him go. He had left me with no choice. One runs a business – and life – on certain principles. That is the way it is. That is how to live a sensible life. Ahmed had left me with no choice but to ask him to leave. But I felt guilty about not even sending him a new year or Diwali or Eid card. Surely I could have done that much!

It was this thought that made me detour to Ahmed's flat on the way back from office that evening. I could have sent him a card, but I thought I would call and give him a box of chocolates. I bought the best box I could from a fancy departmental store. When I re-entered the car, I put it down next to the tiffin carrier on the front seat, close to the driver. I was taking the halwa and nimkis to the missus. As I reclined at the back and the driver revved the engine, it struck me that the chocolates had no smell. What a contrast to the halwa! I remarked jocularly on this to the driver: 'Isn't it funny, Hari, that the sweets the firangs make hardly smell of anything, and the ones we make are so fragrant? I cannot smell these chocolates at all next to the halwa.'

Hari said, frowning slightly, 'I had a cold last week, sir. I think my sense of smell has not come back yet. I cannot smell anything.'

I did not give much thought to his response and recommended a potion to him.

It took us a while to find Ahmed's colony. My memories from that stormy night were of little help once we reached the area. But I had the address, and Hari knew the area better than I did. We did find it after stopping to ask three people and driving back and forth in the neighbourhood for about twenty minutes.

By then it was around seven in the night. As Hari turned the car into the driveway of Ahmed's colony, I was struck by how dimly lit it was. I had obviously not noticed this on the night of the storm. But now I could see that the colony was lit with low-wattage bulbs, glowing a weak yellow and failing to dispel the darkness from most corners and nooks. In my neighbourhood, we are used to huge vapour lamps that turn night into day. This difference made the place seem even sadder and poorer than it had on my last visit.

I recognized the spot where we had parked. I asked Hari to stop there and, picking up the box of chocolates, went to the stairs. The half-broken mailboxes were still there, one of them bearing Ahmed's name. I ascended the stairs slowly. Now that I was there, I was uncertain whether I wanted to see Ahmed again. Can one ever go back to the past anyway, I asked myself. Why disturb the past? But I was holding the box of chocolates, which gave me a sense of purpose, and I continued up the stairs.

Ahmed's flat was locked. Not just locked as it had been last time, with a key; it was bolted from the outside. There was a huge steel lock – brand new from the look of it – hanging on the outside. A part of me was relieved; the closer I had ascended to his flat, the more reluctant I had become to enter it again. A recollection of that sensation from the last time had returned to me, that feeling of entering a different medium, something slower, denser, more resistant. Thank God the place is locked, I remember thinking; now, I can just leave the box for Ahmed, and head home.

But leaving the expensive box outside his door would not be safe, I thought, not in a neighbourhood like this. It would probably be purloined before Ahmed returned. The double lock suggested he intended to be gone for some time.

Then I thought of his neighbours, the Sens. What had Devi said? Something about how they were an ailing, lonely couple and Ahmed often looked after them, did their shopping, fetched the doctor. 'They love him as a son,' Devi had said. I remembered the line. Surely they would be happy to take my box and pass it on to Ahmed?

I turned to the other door on the landing and pressed the buzzer. There was no response. I waited and pressed it again. Just as I was about to turn around, I heard someone fumbling with the latch. The door opened slowly. A small, wizened old man, wearing a banian and dhoti, peered out from behind thick bifocals. 'Yes?' he said suspiciously, in a querulous treble 'What do you want?'

'It is about Ahmed,' I explained.

The man opened the door another inch.

'Are you family?' he asked.

I explained who I was.

He turned around and said something in Bangla, which I do not understand, to someone else in the room. A woman answered him. He opened the door and gestured for me to enter. A rather fat woman, of about his age, was sitting on a sofa in the room. She made an attempt to get up, but it was mostly for show, out of politeness, and remained where she was. Mrs Sen, I told myself.

'Come in, sit down,' she said to me in a loud deep voice. 'So you heard?'

They could read the question from my expression: heard what?

'You don't know?' the woman asked.

'I just came to pay Ahmed a visit,' I replied.

'He doesn't know,' the old man said.

'No, he doesn't,' the woman replied.

'You see …' Mr Sen began.

'Let the man sit down first,' Mrs Sen interrupted him.

I sat down in a chair.

'You see …' Mr Sen began again.

'Let me tell him,' Mrs Sen ordered. Then she turned to me and stared. Her eyelids fluttered as if from an irritation. She licked her lips. She spoke suddenly, abruptly: 'He had been wasting away for some months, but looked strangely happy, almost as if he was bathed in an invisible light. He mostly stayed in the flat, but when he came out on occasion to sit in the sun, he would be talking and laughing to himself. As he often did, but a bit more so, more oblivious of others. Nothing obviously wrong with him though. Just two or three days before he, you know, before he, well, he had knocked an evening or two before that day. That was the last time we saw him. He had a heaped plate of nimkis for us. "I was making some for a very dear friend," he said to me, "and I made too many." Nothing wrong with him but there was a mesmeric look on his face, as I told Mr Sen, who of course cannot see more than a foot in front of him. Then one morning the cleaning woman could not get in. The flat was locked from the inside. When she did not get a response in the afternoon either, some neighbours fetched the spare key he always left with us and opened the door. He was lying in bed, eyes open, with something like a grin on his face. It was unearthly,' she said, and as suddenly as she had spoken, she started sniffing into a handkerchief. 'Such a quiet man, so helpful …'

Mr Sen patted her on a shoulder. There, there, he said. She shrugged off his hand.

It took me a while to figure out this had happened seven days ago. Ahmed had been buried within twenty-four hours, in keeping with Muslim traditions, Mr Sen informed me. There had been no family members. The neighbourhood had taken care of it. And now his flat was to be rented out again.

'That greedy landlord,' Mrs Sen sniffed. 'He put a lock on it, as if the furniture was his, the moment they took poor Ahmed out.'

'We had hoped you were family,' Mr Sen explained in his treble. 'You could have taken the landlord to court.'

The fragrance hit me like a blow to the face when I returned to the car and Hari opened its door for me. Hari saw me wince, and he asked me if I was fine. 'It's nothing,' I assured him, 'I just remembered some work.'

But what I had remembered, if I had ever forgotten it, was the time when I had failed to see or smell the halwa. Ahmed had been alive then, sitting in front of me, eating. The open window, the pool of water on the floor. His mother's face from the wall, with the stare that said I know you, *but* I do not hold anything against you.

What was it, I wondered as I stooped into the car: had I been prevented by the closeness of life from seeing and tasting the halwa that time, and had the distance of death enabled a connection that life no longer allowed? All along, I had seen the failure as Ahmed's: why did he have to insert me into his madness, I had asked. But what if the failure was mine?

What if it was *my* failure to see, feel, smell, touch – a lack Ahmed could not have imagined or expected after all those years we had shared?

I dropped off Hari at a bus stop, telling him I would drive home myself and giving him two days' leave. Then, I texted the missus that something urgent had come up and I needed to make a quick outstation trip. She was not surprised; it has happened in the past. Business comes first in such cases.

I thought I had to be alone in solid, rational surroundings. The container was still in the car, filling it with its smells from a wondrous, forgotten, dense earth.

Which is why I checked into this hotel – what's more solid and rational than an international five-star chain? But I could not rest in my room.

I came down to the bar and found a stranger, lonely like me. We exchanged smiles and names, though perhaps he, like me, assumed a name. We bought each other drinks. Believe me, I did not look like that ancient mariner of the poem we had read in school. Glittery eyes and all. But I must have frightened him anyway. He started looking uneasy when I told him about the tiffin carrier in my car, how it had appeared out of nowhere in my office.

I asked him: what do I do with that tiffin carrier with the ghostly halwa? What happens when I open it for the missus – or for you – and you see nothing, you smell nothing. What happens to me then? Can I trust myself any longer? Shouldn't I fire myself in that case, dismiss myself like I sacked Ahmed, politely but definitively, for how can a person who eats and smells invisible sweetmeats run a successful business in a rational manner? I do not even dare open the tiffin carrier in front of you – or anyone else. I do not dare take the risk!

Ignore it, I had hoped he might say. But I knew I could not ignore it: the smell filled my mind even at the bar. I could not talk about it to anyone I know, for then … then, that person would be like I was in Ahmed's flat that night of the deluge. That is why I had to talk to a stranger at the bar.

But he was not strange enough. He started squirming on the stool. He mumbled something about it getting late, and went away, leaving his beer half-drunk.

I do not blame him: we all hang on to thin spider threads of sanity, swinging over a chasm, and I had not even told him anything about Ahmed. How could he begin to understand? He sidled away, abandoning his Kingfisher. But I could not stop. I had to tell my story.

I went to the reception and got reams of paper from them, and two extra pens, just in case. I had an idea. I had a hope. I knew I had to find the perfect stranger to listen to my story. I returned to my room and started writing.

The thick curtains helped. The 'Do Not Disturb' sign that I hung from my door handle helped. I know that there has been light for a few hours now. But the curtains have kept the room dark, and I have been sitting here, at the desk, in a small pool of light, writing, writing, writing.

My right hand is almost cramped. The story is all told, though I do not know if it is my story or Ahmed's, or whether, as I believed once, we even have separate stories. I will find a title for it, because I am the sort of man who likes to label and file. I will put all these sheets in a folder, if I can find one, and put the folder in the drawer that contains the hotel's copy of the *Bible* and the *Bhagavad Gita*. You I can talk to, for you will not even meet me. We won't know each other.

You will stay in this room after I have left, and the women have cleaned it up, smoothened all the sheets, replenished the bar, restocked the bathroom with its little bottles of shampoo and conditioner. You will open the drawer, and read my story, or maybe you will let it stay, to be read by the next guest, or perhaps one of the management staff. Whoever it may be, you will be a total stranger. That is best. Absolute strangers do not need to stop and greet. But sometimes they do. Wasn't that why the ancient mariner had to address strangers too? How can the strange be narrated except to a stranger?

Ignore my story if you want, stranger, but I cannot ignore it. And I cannot share it in my normal world either. That tiffin carrier with the fragrant halwa will not leave me alone; I know it will come back next Shab-e-baraat if I try to ignore it. I need to solve this; I have to find a solution to it. Perhaps you, in your remoteness, will be my solution. Maybe it is a kind of redemption to speak, freely and truly, to a total stranger? Maybe there is no other redemption? I will find out. I hope to find out.

And then I might also find out why, as I came down the stairs from Ahmed's flat that evening, what I felt was a vague guilt, like a bony hand clutching at my heart – not the rational irritation I had felt on the previous occasion, or even fear, as one should dread the irruption of the past into the present, the dead into life. Was that why I left the box of chocolates outside Ahmed's door, locked as it was, bending to place it carefully, with both hands, as if it was an offering to something unknown and unknowable?

Also by Tabish Khair

NOVELS

An Angel in Pyjamas

The Bus Stopped

Filming: A Love Story

The Thing About Thugs

How to Fight Islamist Terror from the Missionary Position

Just Another Jihadi Jane (Published as *Jihadi Jane* in India)

POETRY

Where Parallel Lines Meet

Man of Glass

STUDIES

Babu Fictions: Alienation in Indian English Novels

The Gothic, Postcolonialism and Otherness: Ghosts from Elsewhere

The New Xenophobia

ANTHOLOGIES

Other Routes: 1500 Years of African and Asian Travel Writing (Co-edited with Justin Edwards, Martin Leer and Hanna Ziadeh)

Reading Literature Today (Co-written with Sebastien Doubinsky)

Transnational and Postcolonial Vampires (Co-edited with Johan Hoglund)

What the Critics Say

'On the surface a book about a bus journey, *The Bus Stopped* is a novel that reflects deeply into the nature and circumstances of human mobility in our modern, unforgiving world' *Outlook*

'[*The Bus Stopped*] is a fine work: short, sweet and brutal' *Sunday Herald*

'Superb ... Elegantly structured and taut with understated passion, *Filming* is a brilliant recreation of the lost world of early cinema and the continuing tragedy of religious hatred. Although set in an India that has now vanished, its delights as well as its message should find admiring readers everywhere' *Independent*

'*Filming* ... [is] ... a multi-narrative that intermixes straight-forward low key story-telling, flashbacks, dream sequences and action shots with admirable élan, unfurling a tale in print that mimics – both in content and in style – the flaming allure of the Indian bioscope...The picture that emerges may sear your soul much like your all-time favourite film' *India Today*

'... an absorbing novel which is distinguished by its ambition, its structural inventiveness and its highly evocative prose' *Times Literary Supplement*

'[*Filming* is a] superb recreation of a lost world' *Tribune*

'Khair's novel [*The Thing About Thugs*] is ingenious and mischievous not only in its powerful subtext about racial profiling but also in its ironic echoes of Charles Dickens and Agatha Christie' *New Yorker*

'A complex, thoughtful novel ... Khair takes two large, mainly invisible cultural narratives ... and blends them in powerful and enlightening ways ... A fascinating and emotionally moving novel for fans of literary fiction' *Library Journal*

'[*The Thing About Thugs*] will have you turning pages feverishly. But be warned: If you want a book with a neatly packaged ending, this isn't it. Rather, its elliptical conclusion is proof positive that when it comes to the really big stories, the ones that define who we are, the telling is never over' Oprah.com and *O Magazine*

'It's easy to see why *The Thing About Thugs* was shortlisted for the Man Asian Literary Prize. Crafted through layers of narrative (third and first-person observations from a variety of characters are interspersed with love letters, passages from Captain Meadows's *Notes on a Thug*, and newspaper clippings), the story both mimics and upends the conventions of a Victorian novel. Tabish Khair also gives voice to a class of Londoner underrepresented in 19th-century-British literature: The voice of the forgotten, the marginalized, the misunderstood, and unknown' *Daily Beast*

'[In *How to Fight Islamist Terror from the Missionary Position*] Khair writes brilliantly about racism, and the misunderstanding between rich and poor. Unmissable' *Times*

'Who wouldn't be struck by a title like this, with its mix of fundamentalism and sniggering sexual reference? Surely, it can only lead to all-title-and-no-trousers disappointment. No, not at all. In fact, the title is nowhere near as irreverent, intelligent, and explosive as the slowly detonated bomb of a story inside' *Independent*

'At less than 200 pages, Khair pulls off a brisk, bitingly funny narrative that manages to make some astute points about both Islamic extremism and the Western penchant for stereotyping without drawing anything like a false equivalence. And for a book so concise and witty, it is also surprisingly textured' *New Republic*

'The message may be serious but the skill and subtlety with which it is delivered, wrapped with so much fun and irreverence, is outstanding. Go get your copy, now' *Asian Age*

'This is a fast-paced, hilarious novel that nonetheless has sufficient depth to withstand several re-readings. If there's any justice, it's going to be … a hit in Euro-America' *Huffington Post*

'Was this intense, enlightening novel [*Just Another Jihadi Jane*] really written not by a British Muslim girl but a male Indian novelist who lives in Denmark? It seems impossible. Required reading for anyone interested in trying to understand our mad, bloody world' *Kirkus Reviews*

'Every step of the way, Khair's gentle humour anticipates and outmanoeuvres the ready prejudices of his characters and readers, indulging and sparing neither' *Guardian*

'*Jihadi Jane* is a disturbing but refreshing read, written with skill and nuance and, more importantly, with wisdom and empathy. It convinces the reader yet again that Khair remains a sterling yet underrated contemporary writer from the Indian subcontinent'
Hindu

'And eventually, it is a testament to Khair's storytelling skills that a reader who feels very differently about faith than Jamilla does should find things to be stimulated and moved by in this story about one woman who finds dramatic redemption and another who is destined to a lifetime of soul-searching' *Open*

'This powerful, compelling, urgent novel succeeds in being compassionate towards its principal characters without flinching from the full horror of their choices' amitavghosh.com/blog